PEN
THE LEGE

O. V. Vijayan (1930–) has published five novels, seven collections of stories, six collections of political essays and one volume of satire. His second novel, *Gurusagaram,* won the National Sahitya Akademi Award. The novel also won the Kerala State Akademi Award and the prestigious Vayalar Award. Vijayan has worked as a political cartoonist for several leading newspapers like the *Hindu, Statesman, Mathrubhumi* (Malayalam) and the *Far Eastern Economic Review.*

Vijayan has translated some of his works into English. These include *The Saga of Dharmapuri* and *After the Hanging and Other Stories,* both published by Penguin.

The Legends of Khasak

O. V. Vijayan

Translated from the Malayalam
by the author

PENGUIN BOOKS

Penguin Books India (P) Ltd., 210, Chiranjiv Tower, 43 Nehru Place, New Delhi 110 019, India
Penguin Books Ltd., 27 Wrights Lane, London W8 5TZ, UK
Penguin Books USA Inc., 375 Hudson Street, New York, NY 10014, USA
Penguin Books Australia Ltd., Ringwood, Victoria, Australia
Penguin Books Canada Ltd., 10 Alcorn Avenue, Suite 300, Toronto, Ontario M4V 3B2, Canada
Penguin Books (NZ) Ltd., 182-190 Wairau Road, Auckland 10, New Zealand

First published in Malayalam by Current Books 1969
First published in English by Penguin Books India (P) Ltd. 1994

10 9 8 7 6 5 4 3 2 1

Typeset in Palatino by Digital Technologies and Printing Solutions, New Delhi

To my father

Contents

Author's Note

THIS IS MY first novel. Written originally in Malayalam as *Khasakkinte Itihasam*, it made its appearance as a serial in the *Mathrubhumi Weekly* in 1968, and as a book in 1969, published by Current Books, Trichur. The actual work on the novel was begun in 1956, and one of its chapters was printed prematurely in the *Mathrubhumi Weekly* in October 1958. The final form of the work was delayed due to a number of reasons. I had become a political cartoonist and was caught up in the compulsions of my new calling. I was also undergoing a painful and long-drawn-out disengagement from communism, which was to bring about subtle but significant changes in narration and characterization. Ravi, the protagonist, who was cast in the mould of the urban revolutionary come to conscientize the village, eventually had to metamorphose into a spiritual wanderer.

It has been difficult translating this book. It is full of dense images of nature, old folk customs, evocations of caste differences, the rich play of dialects, all of which are difficult to render into English. So much has been lost, there was no way it could have been salvaged. I have tried to make the narrative depend on its own energy as much as possible, and preserved the pace and rhythm of the original.

The book in Malayalam currently published by D.C. Books, Kottayam is now in its fourteenth impression.

*

For helping with the making of this translation, there are some people I'd like to thank. First, my nephew, Paul Vinay Kumar, for keeping track of the translation schedules, maintaining the sheaves of paper in order, and also volunteering to be a critical first listener.

Also, Ms Shobha Ramachandran for typing out the novel without errors.

In Search of the Sarai

WHEN THE BUS came to its final halt in Koomankavu, the place did not seem unfamiliar to Ravi. He had never been there before, but he had seen himself coming to this forlorn outpost beneath the immense canopy of trees, with its dozen shops and shacks raised on piles; he had seen it all in recurrent premonitions—the benign age of the trees, their riven bark and roots arched above the earth.

The other passengers had got off earlier and Ravi had sat alone in the bus, contemplating the next part of the journey as one does an ominous transit in one's horoscope . . . . The ride was long and gruelling. Ravi had left Swami Bodhananda's Ashrama very early in the morning to be on time for the cross-country bus. He had woken only the Ashrama's handyman, and of course the Swamini, one to carry his scant luggage and the other for a hurried farewell. Unwittingly he had wrapped her saffron dhoti round his own waist. He had realized the awkward mistake only after he had come a good way. The morning star had risen. On either side of the footpath, tree and shrub and crag had seemed alive in the thinning mist, like breathing embryos.

'Here is someone to carry your luggage,' the conductor said to Ravi.

Ravi stepped out of the bus, still wrapped in thought; and the earth seemed to slip away from under his feet.

A breeze rustled the banyan leaves.

The box and bedroll were hauled down from the roof of the bus. Ravi fixed his gaze on a patch of grime on the bedroll; everything else dissolved round him in a sensuous eddy.

'Where to?' asked the old luggage-carrier who had waited patiently for the young man to come out of his reverie.

'Oh,' said Ravi, 'to Khasak.'

The old man was about to lift the luggage, when Ravi told him to wait. 'Someone's selling sherbet there, let us refresh ourselves.'

The old man declined with peasant ceremony, but Ravi took him along anyway to the shack that sold sherbet. Ravi asked for the drink and sat on the bench in front of the shop, which too was a fixture on piles. He looked around, taking in the scene; the road ended in a circular path of turf, encircling which stood the mounted shacks. Behind them were mud houses lost in the green of planted vegetation—pulses and plantain, and gourds which ripened on thatches.

The sherbet vendor had washed the glasses and uncorked the syrup when Ravi, from habit, asked for ice. The vendor smiled and said, 'You won't need any ice, sir.' True, Ravi realized as he took a sip. The earthen pot had chilled the water and given it the tangy taste of the monsoon's first shower. Ravi sat over another drink and desultorily scanned the knick-knackery in the shack. Behind the vendor's perch hung a large print depicting the tortures of hell. Has that print lain in wait for me, Ravi wondered, behind crazed jars and gothic lemonade bottles with deep green irises? In a corner was a phonograph with a little dog embossed on its horn; mists of memory rose from its damp, rusted flues and spoke to Ravi in sad and tender voices.

'Where might you be going?' asked the vendor.

'Khasak.'

'Visiting relatives?'

'No. I'm going there to teach.'

"Teach? In Khasak? There isn't a school there, at least there wasn't till the other day—'

'One of the District Board's new single teacher schools. I am supposed to get it started.'

The vendor paused, took a closer look at the traveller, and said, 'Thought you were in the Congress.'

His eyes were on Ravi's saffron dhoti. Congress partisans who roamed the countryside during the freedom struggle wore homespun dhotis dyed saffron; many still wore them as a fad.

'Not at the moment,' Ravi said, laughing, 'and this isn't Congress saffron, it is saffron from an Ashrama.' At the mention of the Ashrama the vendor's palms joined in involuntary salutation . . . .

Ravi set out. The old man led the way. They left the bazar of shacks behind them and walked along a lane cut between deep embankments which soon opened out into a valley. Wild tulsi scented the air.

'How far is it, dear Elder?'

'Just a little walk.'

'Is the load heavy?'

'Loads are loads always.'

'We can take turns, I'd like to help.'

It was noon and the wind lay spent over the swooning earth.

Ravi's memories of his childhood always began with

noontide. He sat alone on the verandah of their house on the hilltop. The hill sloped down in flanks of shimmering yellow grass to the valley of coffee below. After the valley, it rose again to the skyline on which diminutive pines swayed in the lucid mirage. His most cherished memory was watching the sky, a pastime in which his mother joined him, though not often as she was big with child. She told him stories of the Devas. These dwellers of the sky drank the milk of the Kalpaka fruit, their elixir of immortality, and flung the empty husks down to the earth. If you gazed on the sky long enough, you saw the husks as transparent apparitions. The sky at noon was full of them. Ravi saw them slide over glistening cloud-hems and pass softly over pine and rock and grass. He watched, leaning on Mother's belly as she reclined on a couch.

'Thirteen!' Ravi whispered, unable to contain his excitement.

'Ah, my child,' Mother said, 'what did you do to them?'

'Counted them, Ma.'

The shy apparitions vanished. The sky was deserted now, save for a lone crested vulture navigating the precipices of space.

'My little star,' Mother said during one such vigil, 'don't lean too hard, you might hurt your sister.'

Little sister, pretty tadpole, who had dreamed and slept long inside Mother's big toe! She had slithered up since to Mother's belly, but he was not fated to see her; Mother took the little one with her on a strange palanquin. Many people moved in and out of the house that day, men who pruned the coffee bushes, nurses who assisted Father in the plantation's infirmary, people he'd never seen before. The palanquin was being readied; Ravi remembered the dirge, the perfume, the flowers and incense. It was noontide, the husks were falling. Mother lay asleep in deep and wondrous peace. As the palanquin rode out of the house, the nurses held him back, gentle hands turned his face away. He did not resist, for he had foreseen this journey down the grass, across the emerald green valley, past the undulant pines.

The covenant ended when his stepmother, his Chittamma, arrived. At noon she had her seista inside, and Ravi sat alone on the verandah, not wanting to watch the sky, uninterested in his toys. Those were his Cinderella days, a period of orphanhood; one day, turning away from the hollows of the sky, he looked towards the miraculous horizon. It was then that they came riding the golden surf of the mirage—the winged and diademed serpents, calling him to play . . . .

'The rains haven't come yet.' It was the old man speaking. 'Maybe the monsoon will fail us this year.'

'Ah, there's no telling.'

'It was floods last year.'

They must have gone about three miles and the old man said there was as much more to go. They had been climbing for some time now, and looking back, Ravi could see the dull little specks that were the roofs of Koomankavu. Ravi paused, the bus was driving back to Palghat town.

'Tired?' the old man asked.

'Oh, no.'

'Something made you sad?'

Ravi smiled. The old man said, 'Let's move on, Kutti.'

The path sloped down again, and Koomankavu was lost to view. The sun had dipped past its zenith; the wind rose again, no longer a gentle breeze but the east wind which blew in through the mountain pass, wild and tumultuous on the palmyra fronds. 'Ah, listen!' said the old man, stopping suddenly in his tracks; a high bird-call above the wind. The Maniyan prophesying rain!

'Perhaps I was wrong about the rains after all,' the old man said with obvious relief. He could go on and on about the rains, the slightest response sustained his animated monologue. The rains, he said, had always tantalized man. 'Isn't that maya, Kutti?' Maya, of course, the cosmic delusion; Ravi knew it was his saffron! For a moment he had a frivolous impulse to play the mystic; he smothered it. No, not on this journey of many lives, this journey of incredible burdens. Let me reach my inn, the village called Khasak. Now Ravi sought to answer the question on maya, 'I suppose so.' The bland answer dampened the old man, but only briefly; soon enough he said, 'They're talking of a dam, but can a dam make the skies rain or turn back the flood?'

Ravi said again, 'Dams do help . . . .'

'One doesn't know,' muttered the old man, 'one doesn't!' He was deeply disturbed by the big machines with arms and mandibles which moved loads of earth and chewed serene rocks into jelly. Could man pit his skills against God's will?

'Here we are, Kutti,' said the old man in pleasant anticipation of laying down the baggage, 'this is Khasak!' As a streamer of cloud moved away, red roof-tiles gleamed through dense greenery. Ravi was aware of a melange of sounds and sights—a mother calling her daughter home, the arcane name stretched out like a melody; whistling pigeons and hosts of other querulous perchers in the green; a water buffalo, its horns raised in alarm at the sight of strangers; the swift-flowing brook, its banks aflame with flowering screw pine; a flight of complaining crows rising in the distance like diminished pterodactyls into the crystal arches of the sun.

Behind Khasak stood the mountain, Chetali, its crown of rock jutting over the paddies below. Wild beehives, one waxed to the other, hung in immense formations underneath the rock, inaccessible to man.

The District Board had leased a house for the school, a modest dwelling of two rooms and corridor, with a large yard shaded by tamarind trees. It stood on the outskirts of the village and belonged to Sivaraman Nair, the impoverished feudal chief of Khasak, who until the last crop, had used the shed to store seedlings. He had been waiting since noon for the teacher's arrival.

'This is our first real school,' he said as he gave Ravi the keys, 'and you are our first schoolmaster, our first Maash.'

Ravi took possession; so this is my transit residency, my Sarai. Ravi went in, the scent of mould and mildew hung heavy.

'It needs living in, Maash,' Sivaraman Nair said, embarrassed about the mildew.

As the school was his property, he had paid for a blackboard, a table and chair, and a couple of benches. To these he had added a personal touch—framed and colourful pictures of Gandhi, Hitler and the monkey god, Hanuman.

'An officer of the Board was here the other day,' Sivaraman Nair said. 'He suggested that you stay in the school. Or else I would have put you up in my own house.'

'I have a lot to thank you for already, Sivaraman Nair. In any case, I wouldn't want to impose myself on you.'

'I hope you'll be comfortable here. If there's anything you need, you can always walk across. My house is just outside the village.'

When the landlord left, a small crowd closed in, boys and girls and women suckling babies. In this crowd stood a dwarf, holding a leash of yarn at the end of which fluttered a green dragonfly. It was hard to tell his age, his torso full grown, hands and legs stunted, his face large with horsey jaws. Ravi didn't want to fraternize too quickly but the children were shoving the dwarf towards him, and so in the age-old colloquy of the primary school he asked, 'What's your name?' The dwarf stood smiling. The children egged him on, 'Tell him, O Kili!' After much cajoling, the dwarf answered in a voice that mixed an old man's gutturals with the lisp of a child, 'Appu-Kili.'

Appu-Kili, Appu-Parrot, the name disarmed Ravi. 'A parrot, are you?'

'Yes, Saar,' the children answered on the dwarf's behalf, volunteering other information too. 'He lisps, Saar. He catches dragonflies, Saar. He likes spiders, Saar.'

'Now go home,' Ravi said. 'See you on Monday. You'll come to school, all of you, won't you?'

The children spoke in chorus, like so many anklets; these silver voices were soon to soothe his sorrow. They replied together, 'We shall come, Saar!' They went off, followed by the women, their breasts spilling out of their babies' lips.

Ravi unpacked his meagre belongings and looked round for places for them; he herded away the reluctant roaches from the window-sill and stacked his books there, pulp and scripture. Settling other odds and ends as best as he could, he sat down on the rickety chair. His calves hurt, his bones ached, the pain travelled through them, travelled dully through his mind . . . .

The rocks were warm with sunset as Ravi walked barefoot

to the brook for a bath. Two women bathed downstream, waists and bosoms covered precariously with towels, their thighs dark in the twilight. Ravi sat on the stream's bed of pebbles with the rich warm rush of the water swirling over his shoulders. The town lay far away in the fading vermilion of the horizon . . . . Ravi turned to look again at Khasak, now starlit with kerosene wicks, and beyond Khasak, at Chetali's looming promontory.

The Second Coming

SEATED IN THE madrassa, Allah-pitcha the mullah taught the children of the Muslims the saga of Khasak. Long, long ago, in times now unknown to man, there came riding into their palm grove a cavalcade of a thousand and one horses. The riders were the Badrins, warriors blessed by the Prophet, and at the head of the column rode the holiest of them all—Sayed Mian Sheikh. An effulgent moon shed its radiance on the thousand steeds of spotless white. But the horse the Sheikh rode was old and ill.

Each generation of young listeners would ask, 'Why an ailing mount, Mollakka?'

And the mullah would repeat, 'Where is succour for the old and dying except in Allah and his beloved Sheikh?'

When the old horse could go no farther the Sheikh signalled his warriors to stop. In the last watch of the night, as the moon set, the faithful animal died and was buried in a palm grove. It is said that he rises from his unmarked grave, rises with the wind, and those who listen in grace can still hear his unsteady footfalls as he canters to the rescue of the lost, often helping them across the wooded mountain pass . . . . The thousand riders dismounted and pitched their camp in the palm grove. The people of

Khasak trace their descent from those one thousand horsemen.

Today the Sheikh sleeps in a rock crypt on top of Chetali. Mortal eyes are yet to discover its exact location. Both the Muslims and the Hindus of Khasak look upon the Sheikh as their protecting deity.

Said the mullah, 'When we grow bent with age, Allah will come and sit on our backs . . . . The Almighty will straddle the infirm and the destitute, as His hosts stand by in veneration . . . .'

The odour of sweat rose from his threadbare shirt and overwhelmed the mullah with the nearness of the Merciful Rider! Like Allah's mangy mount, the mullah looked round at his pupils gathered in the madrassa and asked, 'Whose turn is it today?'

The children brought the mullah's breakfast by turns; it was Kunhamina's turn that morning. Her mother had made vellayappams, rice pancakes puffed with sweet-sour palm toddy, rolled them in banana leaves and stuffed the package into the girl's satchel. Kunhamina's way to the madrassa lay through a patch of woodland, where a clump of Arasu trees shed their flowers over the footpath. That day it had looked as if the trees had rained flowers; Kunhamina had stood admiring the floral carpet, when a flock of foraging peafowl swooped down around her. Charmed, and hardly realizing what she was doing, Kunhamina had undone the package, broken the pancakes into flakes, and fed them to the peafowl. When she had done with the last bit, she had rubbed her palms clean and turned to go. But the crested king-fowl had hopped behind her for more.

'Finished, Peacock-Saar!' she had said. The bird had chased her and pecked her on the calf. It had hurt and bled a little, but she was jubilant, she had something to tell them at the madrassa; she had been pecked by a real peacock! She told Kholusu and Noorjehan.

The spell was broken when the mullah asked whose turn it was. The preening imperial peacock and the rain of flowers vanished; Kunhamina stood up, a delinquent ten-year-old amid the cacophony of the madrassa. The mullah rose and came over to her. The children watched the mullah's cane, and grew tense. But the priest did nothing, he just stood there, lost to the world around him . . . .

Allah-Pitcha's mind went back to the panchayat of the week before, to which he had summoned the Muslim elders. They had come, their beards dyed red to show their orthodoxy. A few young men had drifted in too. They had all gathered beneath the banyan tree which stood at the centre of the village square. The mullah, seated on the brick-paved platform around the foot of the tree, had spoken to his congregation of the perils of the new school, its angular letters and its reckoning—forbidden usury. The mullah had evoked fearsome visions of the insanity of the new learning, the anger of the Sheikh and his second coming. Khasak had two schools—the madrassa where the mullah taught the Koran, and the ezhutthu palli, literally the house of writing, run by a family of hereditary Hindu astrologers. The schools never competed.

At the panchayat there had been whispers of dissent from the young.

'Speak out!' the mullah had said.

'It struck me,' young Kassim had said, 'if the sarkar sets up the school, who among us can wish it away?'

Kuppu-Acchan, the village gossip perched on the

granite ledge in front of Aliyar's teashop, known in common parlance as a load-rest (on which pack-carriers rested their loads) had said to no one in particular 'What do you people say? Will it work?

The school was not without its partisans—Sivaraman Nair the landlord his nephew Madhavan Nair the village tailor Zulfiqur Hayat the cousin of the first native to trade beyond the frontiers of Khasak. Kuppu-Acchan had altered his position to catch the attention of a passing red-beard, 'Who can run this school if the people don't care for it?' Hardly had he finished this taunt when Sivaraman Nair, bare-chested, a bunch of keys hanging from his girdle as the landlord's insignia, had come up to Kuppu-Acchan's perch and whispered, 'Kuppu, remember your promise, won't you?'

'You can depend on Kuppu, Venerable Nair.'

'Ten admissions . . . .

'It's done.'

'Can you make it fifteen?'

'Be at peace, Venerable Nair. A promise is a promise.'

'The school will need many more than fifteen children to save it from closing down.' Sivaraman Nair had drawn closer, 'The Bouddhas* are against us.'

With a discreet wink Kuppu-Achchan had alerted the landlord that the Bouddha elders were headed this way after the panchayat. Leading them was Allah-Pitcha. The mullah had entered Aliyar's teashop with a few elders who were his confidants, and since there wasn't room enough, the rest of the crowd had remained in front of the shop. The mullah had asked one of the elders, 'So, it's true?'

---

* **Though literally Bouddha meant a follower of the Buddha, Hindu upper castes used it loosely for any other religionist, here the Muslim.**

'True,' the elder had answered.

The mullah had muttered in disbelief, 'Nizam Ali is back . . . . Where is he?' The mullah had said this in a dull, barely audible tone. The listening elders had been distressed.

The Story of the Return was put together from its fragments. Nizam Ali had arrived four nights ago, walked over marsh and scrub and disappeared into the Mosque of the King, a haunted ruin.

'He has made it his home,' the villagers told one another, 'he has tamed the spirits.'

None of these accounts had reached the mullah but memories had flooded the old man's mind, unbecoming memories, of a boy of sixteen with a girl's lips and curls like tendrils that framed his face. This was no time to reminisce, but to confront the heresy; Nizam Ali had come back to Khasak as the self-proclaimed Khazi, the sorcerer of the Sheikh, an authority never known in the village before. The mullah had asked again, petulant as a child, 'Why did no one tell me? No one among you . . . .' The old red-beards wouldn't reply. 'And you, Aliyar?' the mullah had picked on the young man who owned the teashop, 'You knew too?'

Aliyar, his protege, had sulked behind the samovar. Suddenly the mullah had felt incapacitated, ahead of him lay an occult duel between priest and pretender. Allah-Pitcha had had these manic fits before, and Thitthi Bi his wife had sorrowed with him, but she had refused to be jealous; jealousy over a boy was unbecoming.

The mullah had stooped over his tea. Insane images rose and fell in his mind—the Khazi destroying the old order, the new school overthrowing hallowed myths, the pinch of the sandal on his big toe turning into a sore that wouldn't go away . . . . The tea had turned cold. The crowd from the panchayat had thinned away, but now another, larger crowd was heading for the teashop, young men and boys moving in fluid circles round their new leader. The mullah had risen and gone out into the yard.

'Nizam Ali!' the mullah was face to face with the apostate.

'Khazi,' his former novice had corrected him sternly. Allah-Pitcha had reeled; finding his voice again he had said, 'Nizam Ali, are you the Truth or the Deception?'

'The Truth.'

The mullah had waited in vain for an augury, the clicking of a lizard, a gust of wind carrying disembodied voices, a scarf of blue cloud across the magic mountain. Feebly, and in pain, he had said, 'Imposter! You are possessed by an unclean spirit.' He had scooped up a fistful of dust, chanted a spell over it and hurled it at Nizam Ali. In the effort of the throw, which missed the Khazi, the mullah had swayed and would have fallen had Aliyar not held him. During all this Nizam Ali had stood his ground smiling.

The mullah, downcast, had gone back into the teashop. He had then asked one of the faithful red-beards, 'Did the erring one speak of the school?'

'He did, and with much vehemence.'

'What did he say?'

'He said that the spirit of the Sheikh was not angered over the school, and that he, the Sheikh's Khazi, would plant the school like a sapling.'

The mullah had sat awhile telling his beads. Then he had spoken, 'In this school our children will be confounded by kafir (infidel) knowledge. How can anyone planting such a sapling be the Sheikh's Khazi?'

The mullah had sipped his tea, now bitter, and in the next instant he had spat it out in a burst of spray. He had turned his fury on Aliyar. 'Dog, shameless dog!' he had screamed. 'Mixing the kafir milk powder in the tea!' Swearing, whimpering, drooling, he had seized cups and glasses and had begun to fling them out into the yard in a frenzy.

'Mollakka!' a cool voice had called to him from the yard. Then Nizam Ali had strode into the teashop, kicking a barricade of benches aside. The mullah had sat down, undone; the intruding sorcerer had loomed over him. He had heard the stern whispered command, 'Calm down, Mollakka!'

In the madrassa, the mullah stood beside the terrified Kunhamina as if in deep meditation, tears wetting his shirt-front. Then laying his hand on Kunhamina's head, he said, 'You won't repeat this, will you, O Bilal?'

'No,' she said.

'Sit down.'

The children were bewildered. Why did the mullah pardon her, why did he stand so long near Kunhamina, and why did he weep?

'And now, tell me,' the mullah said, 'will you go to the kafir's school?'

Grateful for the reprieve, Kunhamina was prepared to promise anything, 'I will not go.'

'Swear by the Sheikh.'

'By the most Holy Sheikh,' and she added on her own, 'by the Badrins, by the Prophet . . .'

'Swear by Mariyamma.'

Mariyamma was the Goddess of Smallpox, worshipped by the Hindu lower castes who appeased her with toddy and obscene song. The mullah was taking no chances.

'By Mariyamma,' the girl chanted, again adding gratuitous divinities to her oath. 'By the goddess on the tamarind branch, by the snake-gods—I will not go to the kafir's school!'

The mullah returned to his low stool, the seat of the chronicler till this his sixtieth year. Forty years he had walked the mountain path, singing the glory of the Sheikh, forty years to infirmity. From the big toe of the wayfarer, the lesion, almost forgotten, sent up its dull signal of pain.

The Priest

TWELVE MOSQUES IN ruin, a desolate ring round the village; in them lay stagnant the infinite time of Khasak. Legend had it that pagan deities sought to rebuild the oldest of them. But the deities were sworn to build only in the dark, and complete their task before day broke. Demon spirits who turned themselves into roosters crowed when it was still night, which confounded the deities, who fled, abandoning the incomplete edifice. A curse lay on the mosques and after the deities were thwarted no one, and certainly no human, could finish building any of the houses of worship, least of all the most ancient of them. If you asked the villagers how old the mosque was, they would reply, 'Millennia.' Through these interminable years the moss had softened the bricks until the mosque was a print of outlines in the marsh.

The twelfth mosque, called the Mosque of the King, was the most recent of the ruins. Its walls and roof covered with picturesque disfigurement, the mosque exuded the dismal well-being of an antique. It overlooked the Araby tank, a pond of crystal water, to which kabandhas, beings dismembered in ancient wars, came to bathe their unhealed wounds. In the thirteenth mosque, Allah-Pitcha led the prayers.

The mullahs of Khasak were a line of foundlings, all adopted in unusual circumstances. So when Allah-Pitcha had come upon the beautiful boy on the slopes of Chetali, he thought his own search for a successor had ended. That was twelve years ago, when his daughter was sixteen. The boy was as old as she, clad in just a torn strip of cloth through which the mullah saw his thighs and their delicate down.

'What brings you to the Sheikh's valley?' Allah-Pitcha had asked.

'Snakes,' the boy had replied. 'I come to catch them.'

'What kind of snakes?'

'The hooded ones, the reptile princes.'

'For what purpose?'

The boy had not answered, he merely stood before the priest and smiled.

'What's your name, O ill-begotten one?' the mullah then asked.

'Nizam Ali.'

'Are your mother and father, Attha and Umma living?'

'Neither of them.'

'A home?'

'None.'

The boy smiled, the ageing priest stroked his dimpled cheek. The mullah had hearkened again, and now there came the sign from Chetali, a wind in the deep dark thickets and a flashing scrub fire which spewed down wisps of cloud-blue smoke over the slope. The priest had stood gazing at the mountain a long while. When his trance ended, he had found the boy still before him, but now he held a green snake writhing in his hand, the snake of the bushes which spat venom into the eyes of the unwary.

'Why didn't you catch the reptile prince?' the mullah had asked.

'Because,' the boy replied, 'even this one can grow to be as venomous.'

'Truly said. But when will that be?'

'When its hour draws near.'

'Let the evil one go back into the bushes for now,' said the mullah.

The boy did as he was told, he let the snake down and it slithered away.

'Now follow me,' the mullah had said. Chanting holy verses Allah-Pitcha had come home with the beautiful boy in tow. That night no one slept . . . . Nizam Ali became part of the family. Thithi Bi would cook buffalo meat and make paththiris, she would spread them before the boy for supper. She would melt lac for him to massage his body with; he would stand amidst lush flower-beds in the evening sun to let the lac sink in and make his skin soft and glowing . . . .

Three years had gone by. One day the mullah had noticed that Nizam Ali's head hadn't been shaven. The devout Muslim shaved his head to distinguish himself from the pagan, and Allah-Pitcha had instructed the Ossan, the Muslim barber, to give his ward the ritual shave on the night of every new moon.

'I see your hair's grown long,' the mullah had said. 'Didn't you go to the Ossan?'

Nizam Ali smiled, 'I forgot.'

'Better have it done soon.'

Allah-Pitcha had had to go to Koomankavu the next day. He had returned at night to find Nizam Ali gazing into Maimoona's cracked mirror; he was carefully tending the incipient curls. The mullah had held back a feeble reprimand . . . . The hair grew on. There were others who weren't kafirs and wore their hair long—Alam, Amir, Mohiyuddin and Attar. Attar had been the first to succumb to temptation. Years ago he had dropped out of the madrassa and become a vagabond. Later he had set up a little business and begun to make money. In the little thatched house he had acquired in Koomankavu which Attar called his 'factory', ten starved and ill-paid men sat from dawn to dusk, rolling beedis. Attar had cast his lot with Iblis the Devil and he wouldn't pay his workers their rightful wages. The mullah had remembered the drop-out with a measure of bitterness and wondered what pestilence he carried in his hair—dandruff, lice? He was determined that that should not be Nizam Ali's way! Thithi Bi had tried to reason with her husband. After all weren't more and more young believers taking to pagan hairstyles without giving up their faith?

'But it's wrong,' Allah-Pitcha had said. 'He is Khasak's next mullah.'

He shook his head and went on in passive misery, 'It's wrong! He's to wed Maimoona.'

The words had spilled out of him, and sounded unreal. In fact Maimoona's wedding was the last thing on his mind; he had been troubled instead by a vision of soft tendrils curling round a face in a mirror, hair more voluptuous than Maimoona's locks, or Thithi Bi's, hair forever growing and reaching out as vile temptation.

Soon the mullah had had another journey to undertake—to the village of Athicode where his second wife lived, whom he never failed to visit once a year. He would be gone for four or five days and, since in Khasak the mullah served as muezzin as well, he entrusted the call for the five namazes to Nizam Ali . . . .

The mullah had returned to find that for five days Khasak had gone without the muezzin's call. The priest was seized with rage, and he had turned on Maimoona.

'Where is he?' the mullah demanded.

'Who, Aththa?'

'You dare ask me who, you Iblis?'

Allah-Pitcha had stormed out of the house and walked straight to the mosque. Black hallucinations had dimmed his sight; there was a noisy wind on the palm fronds. He had climbed up to the disused storey, where it was dark both night and day. Tiny bats flew in frenetic circles, screeching. On the balcony, fists clenched and pressed against his temples lest the veins in them burst, the mullah had let out a long cry: *Allaho Akbar! Allaho Akbar! Ashahado Inna la Ilaha Illallah!* It was between the fajir and zohar namazes, between the morning and the forenoon prayers, an untimely call. It reverberated through Khasak, a cry of sorrow.

The mullah had sat down drained, trembling, on the cold dark floor, calming himself with his beads. After a while, he had risen and walked over the grasslands between the mosque and the village. In the mosque's graveyard he had seen Nizam Ali, seated on a gravestone, basking in the heat, his hair like a halo in the sun.

Nizam Ali had not come home for supper that night, and the mullah himself had sat on the steps, disinclined to eat. Tired of waiting for her husband, Thithi Bi had ladled out wet, sour rice in a china bowl. 'Maimoona,' she had said in a whisper, 'take this to Attha.'

Maimoona had spread the little mat on the floor of the corridor and lit the wick lamp. 'Attha!' she had called, timidly. There was no answer. Maimoona had set the bowl down near the mat and withdrawn silently. Neither woman dared intrude on these rare moments of rage of the old man. Presently they had heard the sound of porcelain shattering. Then they had heard his footfalls recede down the corridor, through the verandah and across the yard.

Thithi Bi had cried herself to sleep, but Maimoona neither cried nor slept. Outside, the moon was full, and the wind blew eddying moonlit mists down the mountain pass. Over its torrent she had heard her father singing in the wilderness the song he had written—a tired, baffled lament:

'I have sung the Bismi
I begin my verse
Allah give me grace
To sing of the Prophet's battles.'

Nizam Ali had left Khasak the next day to become a beedi-roller in Attar's 'factory'.

The Houri of Khasak

AFTER HE LEFT Khasak, Nizam Ali never stepped into the village again; nor did the mullah enter Koomankavu on his rambling journeys. Nizam Ali kept himself to the run-down shed which was Attar's 'factory', where ten workmen sat rolling beedis. Attar and his wife lived in the mud-walled house behind the shed. Nizam Ali rolled faster and better than the nine others. Stooped over his bamboo tray, he worked into the small hours, and never asked for higher wages, all of which pleased Attar who fed him and let him sleep in the shed. Two years went by and, for the mullah, the distance between his home in Khasak and the workhouse in Koomankavu became a chasm he dared not cross. Thithi Bi saw her daughter growing up, maturing visibly each day, impatient and challengingly beautiful like no woman Khasak had seen. Thithi Bi pleaded with her husband, 'Go one day to Koomankavu and talk to the boy. We are old, mellow enough to forgive.' There was no pride left in the mullah, only sorrow. He muttered a now familiar chant, 'It'll never be the same again!'

Thithi Bi had never seen her husband so broken; she saw in his pouchy eyes and drawn cheeks the first signs of aging. He had frequent fevers nowadays. She told herself that she would feed him medicated chicken broth once the rain settled to a healing tenor; but she also knew she might never be able to put by enough coppers for the price of chicken.

'Just once,' she repeated, 'try and visit him there.'

In a voice full of tenderness he said, 'No, Thithi Bi.' She had never heard this voice before, the new assonance in which he called her name. It touched her deeply. She came over and sat beside him, and put her fair arms around his shoulders. Later, when she went to the backyard to tend the plantains, she saw Maimoona coming home with a pitcher of water. Her thattan, the traditional scarf with which Muslim women covered their hair, had slipped; it hung limply behind her. This was apostasy. But the thattan was more than an observance; women's hair, if left uncovered, brought astral beings down in lust. Of course the kafir women walked about with their hair uncovered, and at times even their breasts bare. Thithi Bi had no doubt that the flying Gandharvas (elves) had sired satanic offspring in them. Maimoona pulled the thattan over her head in casual deference to the presence of her mother. It slipped again, as casually. Thithi Bi did not admonish her, but gazed helplessly on this devastating beauty born of her flesh.

Maimoona walked with power and abundance, sleeves rolled up to bare her arms, revealing the translucent skin beneath which the blue veins were a gorgeous filigree. Often Maimoona turned her charms on her pursuers, reducing them to blushing boys. She was the sacrificial mare no one could lasso.

In the fifth year of his migration to Koomankavu, Nizam Ali set up his own enterprise with two hired hands. It was rumoured that Attar's wife had given him the money to get started, though no one knew for certain. But Attar and his wife had had a noisy row out in the street.

Bidis came in conical packs of ten, and though it was the same tobacco wrapped in the same leaf, the innumerable little 'companies' sported their own labels, and connoisseurs staked their preferences for their favourite brands. Attar's pack of ten had around it a band of coloured paper on which was printed Attar's photograph with the legend, *God bless M. Attar Photo Bidi.* It had cost Attar time and money. He had gone to Palghat town to get himself photographed in a hired coat and tie and fez. Attar's wife had said he appeared uncomfortable in print but Attar was obsessed with his picture. Sometimes, overcome with this self-love, Attar would go behind overgrown thickets and in that privacy commune with his own printed face, secretive and sorrowful, captured with such fidelity in black and violet printer's ink.

For seven years Attar's bidi had been popular in those parts. Now the upstart was challenging him by entering the fray with his own trade mark, *Sayed Mian Sheikh bless Nizam Photo Bidi.* And the maverick brought to the battle something Attar had not dreamt of—advertising! On the walls of Koomankavu, on the little culverts, across quarried rocks, misspelt slogans in large letters appeared overnight, emblazoned with turmeric and charcoal, *Nizam Photo health-giving. Makes you hungry, incinerates even putrid food stuck in the gizzard!* Under cover of night Nizam Ali had hundreds of his bidi wrappers scattered along the footpaths and in the morning the campaign burst upon the villagers. Maimoona picked one up and treasured it; how different, she thought, from the tense and ugly Attar! Nizam Ali smiled in print with the ease of one born to it, his mouth seductive, curls of hair down his temples in blue rolls, his shirt unbuttoned.

Then the exile ended. Nizam Ali came to Khasak during the Eid festival, dressed in colourful silk, his broad, many-pocketed canvas belt showing through a diaphanous shirt, identical red scarves round the head and neck and peeping out of the breast pocket, sandals on his feet that were designed to squeak while walking, and a long electric torch flaunted at midday as a symbol of prosperity. Nizam Ali, now Nizam Ali Muthalali, an owner of wealth, mingled with the admiring crowd. Kassim and Haneefa, Ubaid Dawood and Ussamat, the smooth-cheeked wastrels of Khasak who trailed the houri these days, faced Nizam Ali in trepidation and hopelessness. Kassim spoke for them, 'Nizam Anno, have you come back for good?'

'What a question!' Nizam Ali said. 'Do you think I could leave my factory to take care of itself?'

Nizam Ali sat on a bench inside Aliyar's teashop, legs crossed in the lotus posture, while an admiring throng fretted in the yard. Nizam Ali Muthalali treated everyone to tea and crisp murukkus.

Great monsoon clouds radiated heat from afar. Maimoona stood in waist deep water, bathing, splashing in the clear waters of the Araby tank. The tank and the Mosque of the King on the rise over it were haunted. In the wars of a different age the Arabs had put renegades and infidels to the sword and flung their dismembered bodies into the tank. Even now the kabandhas were believed to return to the tank in the dense night and at desolate noontide. Maimoona bathed alone, bare-breasted, and watched the soap bubbles wink red and blue. In the paddies far away two women were transplanting seedlings, there was no one else in sight. The wind was still, the mirage swelled in tides over the banyans. Maimoona climbed out of the water and walked up the rise, the wet clothes clinging to her body; she trod on thorns but felt no pain on this delirious journey. It was dark inside the Mosque of the King, yet she made out the looming silhouette that stood waiting.

'You will catch a cold in these wet clothes,' Nizam Ali said, 'put them away.'

The news stunned Khasak: Maimoona was to be married off!

In the congregations beneath the banyan and in Aliyar's teashop there was utter disbelief. Every man in the village had bound this mare in his fantasies . . . . The wedding guests gathered as for a funeral. The knock-kneed groom tottered in, his jowls thrown into waxen relief by the wedding shave: Chukkru the diver, called 'Diving Fowl' in Khasak and the adjoining countryside, felt neither joy nor anxiety as the mullah made him chant the verses which gave him for wife the houri of Khasak.

That night a frenzied traveller stalked out of Khasak. No one saw him go. It was a night blacker than other nights, the skies low, laden with the imminent monsoon. The traveller caught glimpses of his path as lightning blazed and exploded. That was no path for men but for djinns and iffriths. Nizam Ali strode on. Chetali was soon far behind him.

After the Lost Years

NIZAM ALI WAS gone, nobody knew where. His two hired hands went on rolling the clumsy little cigarillos, but there was nobody around to give them wages. After a week they shut down the 'factory', and morose and masterless, sought other employment. One joined Attar and the other took to illicit distilling.

Two years after his mysterious disappearance Nizam Ali strolled into Koomankavu's bazar as if he had never been away. He went up to Attar and asked coolly, 'Can I work for you?' Attar could have killed him for all those private and rancid humiliations. Instead he chose a devious path. He took Nizam Ali in so that he could harrass him at will, so he could withhold his wages and watch him survive on the meagre food the teashops served, so he could singe the locks and starve the seducer's face thin. And indeed wear him down in many other ways.

'Very well,' Attar said, 'but I don't want any more nonsense.'

'Of course not,' Nizam Ali replied, 'and when Nizam promises, the promise is kept.'

'You can't sleep in the factory like you used to. Look out for a place.'

'Nizam is like the wind. He blows, he dies down.'

'Stop this loose talk.'

'Certainly.'

Later that evening Attar's wife Sohra Bi, trying to sound casual, said to her husband, 'They say he has grown his hair long like a woman.'

'Shut up, you bitch!' Attar exploded.

Nizam Ali kept his word. In a frenzy that baffled even Attar, he rolled twice as many bidis as the others did, bidis of perfect tautness. Attar watched those beautiful fingers working in a rage . . . . Months went by, and the rage abated. Then a small red board appeared on the door of Nizam Ali's one-room hut. Scribbled in tar across the red was this legend: *Koomankavu Bidi Workers' Union.* Seven of Attar's workmen joined the Union. These men gathered at odd places, secretive and wise; partisans from Palghat town came to them and read out dim prophecies. They said a spectre was haunting Europe. 'Do you know what a spectre is?' the ideologues asked the bidi-rollers.

'We know, comrades,' Koomankavu's new proletarians replied. 'We have djinns and poothams (demons) here.'

'You are not listening, comrades.'

'There are even more spectres in Khasak than . . . .'

On the twenty-first of January they observed Lenin's birth anniversary; on another day a dozen men marched in procession, the first procession Koomankavu had seen.

Muslim trade-unionists visited Attar and told him these processions were evil and their slogans satanic. The right-wing Congressmen had an even more scary story, they said the Russians were coming. Attar listened quietly. He knew better, it was a private knowledge he chose not to share with anybody. It was more a war of the spirit than of class. Attar had struggled hard to make his money—God was his witness—and with that money he had built an attic over his tiny home. The second storey was the signal to all men that he was a muthalali, an owner of wealth. 'Malika' was the name of the two-storeyed house, and from that he took the 'M' that was to precede his name, M. Attar, Malikakkal Attar Muthalali, the one who lived in the two-storeyed house. He ignored the satanic peril, and worried even less about the Russians. All that mattered to him now was the invisible enemy which was forever seeking to push him back over the brink, to his childhood of poverty. Attar had resisted, now he would overcome. This was the heroic hour.

He dismissed Nizam Ali.

With that the strike began. Back in Khasak, the people looked on in fascination and concern at this war between their expatriates. Processions went round Koomankavu, went round and round not knowing where to go. All old red lungis were torn into flags for the processionists, and the vanguard carried the Koran and a portrait of Stalin. Slogans ripped the peace of Koomankavu:

'Anglo-American exploitation—Murdabad!'

'Oppressor M Attar—Murdabad!'

'Inquilab—Zindabad!'

Tanka, who carried basketfuls of jaggery from Khasak to Koomankavu, was witness to all this and brought some of the insurrection home.

'Can you guess who leads it all?' She was ecstatic. 'It is him!'

'Naizam Annan?' asked Maimoona.

'Yes, my houri.'

Maimoona giggled and reddened . . . The insurrection took a grave turn on its fifth day when Attar thrashed a striking worker and badly bruised him. Attar himself was satisfied that he had acted within the hallowed laws of property and awaited the arrival of the police with much optimism. The police came in khaki fatigues and red berets. Attar had no doubt they would compliment him for what he had done for the law. He went out to receive them. They promptly arrested him and Nizam Ali and took them in handcuffs to Palghat town. The 'factory' collapsed, creditors seized the stock of bidis and unrolled tobacco. Soon a big manufacturer from Palghat town opened a branch in Koomankavu. With that ended both the insurrection and Attar's dreams of a trading dynasty.

Nizam Ali lay beaten black and blue inside a police cell. He rose with the dawn winds in a slow resurrection. The charges against him were grievous—collusion with a foreign power, war against the state, incitement to murder. Nizam Ali found all this ignominy bearable, but not the pain which alternated with merciful patches of oblivion. Through the rhythms of pain and blankness, this question nagged him—what were the police doing in his war with the mullah?

Dawn lit the cells. Nizam Ali levered himself up by holding on to the prison bars. He heard the cock crow outside and for a moment gave himself the freedom to fantasize—was this the bird of dawn crowing from Khasak? With a great effort he kept standing and hailed the first policeman who passed, 'Yajaman, I have a request, a humble prisoner's request.'

'Let's hear it.'

'I want to speak to the Inspector-Yajaman.'

Nizam Ali found himself standing on shaky legs before the Inspector.

'Yajaman,' Nizam Ali said, 'I quit all this.'

The Inspector eyed the prisoner with curiosity.

'Wisdom dawns late,' he said. 'Isn't that so?'

'Yes, Yajaman. Such is maya.'

This surely was a political detenu with a difference. The Inspector smiled, 'Maya?'

'Yes, Yajaman. The unreal aspect of things. But the maya has ended. The Old One visited me in the cell last night.'

'The Old One? In the cell?'

'Yes, Yajaman. Sayed Mian Sheikh.'

The Inspector turned to the constable.

'What's this I hear? Someone in the cell, without permission . . . .'

The constable was puzzled. Nizam Ali hastened to intervene, 'Yajaman, it is a djinn, a ghost . . . .'

The Inspector sighed in relief, leaned back in his chair and spoke to the constable in admonition, 'You men will never learn! Must you beat them on the head?' Turning to Nizam Ali who stood in a trance, the Inspector said, 'Sit down on the chair. Now will you make us lock you up again?'

'Insha Allah, there will be no more trouble on my part. Mian Sheikh will guide me wisely.'

'Who? The ghost?'

'Yes, Yajaman.'

'Now listen, Ali. I shall read out this statement to you. Will you sign it?'

'Yes, Yajaman.'

The Inspector took out a frayed yellow sheet from a pile of government stationery, and wrote out a document for the renegade: I, Nizam Ali, do hearby pledge to eschew violence and to work for a change of government only through constitutional means, and . . . .

Nizam Ali held out his left thumb which the Inspector inked on the stamp pad. When the thumb impression was made, Nizam Ali said hesitantly, 'A request . . . .'

'Certainly,' the Inspector said.

'Below my name and thumb impression . . . .'

'Yes, Ali?'

'Add the word Khazi.'

'Certainly. But what does that mean?'

'The Old One ordained me last night, I am his Khazi from now on.'

The Inspector felt expansive as one does when dealing with the gently insane.

'As you wish, Ali,' he said. 'Now get back to your cell and relax. Tomorrow or the day after we'll drop the charges.' And he turned to his constable, 'Get some herbal oil and bathe him in plenty of cold water.'

Nizam Ali cast his dusky eyes on the Inspector and chanted a benign spell, *'Al Hamdo Lillahe Rabbil Aalemeen. Ar Rahmanir Rahim. Malike Yaumiddin . . . .'*

Nizam Ali walked over the rocks of Chetali with the crisp tread of a mountain goat. He sensed the nearness of the forbidden beehives, he bowed before the crypt from which the Sheikh rose to protect the living and the dead of Khasak. Nizam Ali stood on Chetali's peak, gazing up, his hands spread like the wings of an eagle. The wind blew free, and marvellous little beings rode past him in flimsy sky-canoes. Nizam Ali leapt up into the sky which seemed within reach, and the next moment he was plummeting down through wind and cloud.

After a while, he rose from the soft damp earth. He did not know how long he had lain there. In great pain he began his walk towards Khasak . . . . His unearthly chant alerted Khasak; some elders caught a glimpse of a gaunt figure walking over the burial marshes and disappearing into the Mosque of the King.

'The Ordination!' the elders whispered among themselves. Word went round of an occult presence in the village, but it did not reach the mullah who was lost in long and solitary prayer in the mosque that night . . . . On the fifth day Nizam Ali strode into Khasak and stood beneath the great banyan. That was the day of Allah-Pitcha's disastrous palaver over the school.

'Why didn't you tell me of his return?' the mullah cried. Ponthu Rawuthar, the elder who was by then his only listener in Aliyar's teashop, merely shook his head in sorrow.

Outside, the Khazi, the first one Khasak ever had, sermonized to the faithful.

The Schools

THE KHAZI WENT among the people, spreading the glad tidings of the Sheikh. The mullah had barred the children from the school, now the Khazi commended its new learning. What was the Khazi's power? What but the miraculous signs? Midnight baths in the cursed tank, the taming of the spirits in marsh and mosque, fetishes scattered amid gravestones.

'What is the Khazi's truth?' the troubled elders asked one another.

They recalled the spell the mullah had tried to cast on Nizam Ali. They had seen the spell fail.

'The Khazi's truth,' they told themselves, 'is the Sheikh's truth.'

'If that be so,' troubled minds were in search of certitude, 'is Mollakka the untruth?'

'He is the truth too.'

'How is it so?'

'Many truths make the big truth.'

In the seedling house, Ravi was trying to calm the landlord who had burst in, greatly agitated.

'The Bouddhas are against us,' Sivaraman Nair whispered.

'Let them be.'

'They are holding the children back.'

'Don't worry.'

Sivaraman Nair quietened, but he was still panting. Then, on second thoughts he said, 'It is just as well, Maash. Better to have them on the other side.'

It was then they saw the lithe figure slouching in the shade of the tamarind tree.

'*Assalam Aleikum*!' the visitor greeted them from a distance.

'*Waleikum Salaam*!' Ravi returned the greeting.

'May I approach?'

'Please do . . . .'

He walked up with a springy stride, a dappled apparition emerging from under the tamarind's porous canopy.

'I am Sayed Mian Sheikh's Khazi.'

'I'm the District Board's schoolmaster,' said Ravi, not quite knowing what to say.

Hair parted and combed down to his shoulders, his locks feminine and dark, the Khazi stood there tall and strangely elegant.

'I bring you Sayed Mian Sheikh's blessings,' the Khazi said. 'Your school will prosper.' And then he was gone as abruptly as he had come.

'Tell me, Sivaraman Nair,' Ravi said, 'who's this Sayed Mian Sheikh?'

Sivaraman Nair was embarrassed; the Sheikh's Khazi pledged Bouddha support to the school at the very moment he was raising the Bouddha issue. Fortunately Ravi was not bothered about these undercurrents of animosity. He was merely curious.

'Don't be afraid, Maash,' Sivaraman Nair said.

'I'm not afraid. But who is he?'

'He is . . . he is a ghost.'

'A ghost!' Ravi laughed and stretched in his chair. He lit a cigarette. Sivaraman Nair did not like this profane disrespect.

'The ghost is real, Maash,' said the landlord, 'and he is a Muslim ghost, an unclean one. But as I've said often, it can't touch us if we Hindus stick together. The Devi of the temple in Kozhanasseri can make this Muslim spirit defecate in terror.'

At that triumphant prospect Sivaraman Nair broke into verse:

> *'It is not the damned shaven head*
> *that will wear the crown of Bharat.'*

He went over it again in silence, and laughed, and said, 'Kalyanikutti, my daughter, taught me these lines, Maash. Isn't the poet right?'

'Absolutely.'

But alone on his way home, Sivaraman Nair turned compulsively to gaze at the mountain; a cloud had darkened the wild beehives . . . . When he reached home, his wife Narayani was on the verandah with nothing on but a wet and threadbare towel round her waist. She was spreading sandalwood paste on her body. As she rubbed the fragrant paste on her breasts and thighs, Sivaraman Nair gazed for one fleeting moment, devastated; Narayani hadn't changed in these thirty years she had been his wife.

She broke off in the middle of the song she was singing and turned to her husband with a caustic welcome, 'Has my Nair's frenzy passed? And how goes the war over the seedling house?'

Sivaraman Nair pretended not to hear, chanted a name of God and walked past her into the house. He called out to his daughter, 'Kalyanikutti, my child, is there something to eat?'

Anklets tinkled down a corridor, then bangles clinked softly, then hands went to work over hearth and vessel.

Narayani was still on the verandah . . . . It had begun thirty years ago, within days of their marriage. Narayani would bare herself to the sunny forenoon winds and smear sandal paste all over her body. Sivaraman Nair had objected. She had done it again. She wore a turquoise pendant over her breasts and walked across the paddies for a bath in the brook, and took a long time to return.

'Where were you all this while?' Sivaraman Nair asked her once.

'The seedling house.'

'What have you to do there?'

'My mother told me paddy mildew is good for the complexion.'

'I know of no such discovery.'

'Mother knows.'

'Let your mother keep her knowledge to herself. You aren't going to that wretched shed anymore.'

But she went again, and again, until Sivaraman Nair confronted her once again.

'Who was it in the tamarind yard of the seedling house?' he asked.

Narayani had looked silently and menacingly into his eyes. Sivaraman Nair repeated, 'Who was it?'

'Kuppu,' she said, 'Kuppu, the palm-climber.'

'What did he come there for?'

'He wanted fire to light his bidi.'

'But where can one find fire in the seedling house?'

The years went by . . . . Sivaraman Nair recalled it all, the mildew on the breasts and the palm-climber's quest for fire. He would look on Kalyanikutti's face, on her eyes and nose and lips, sometimes in frozen horror, sometimes in sad and forgiving love.

There was an upper-primary school in the adjoining village, one that taught bad English and arithmetic, but this did not worry the mullah, as he was certain that not many Muslim children would walk two miles across shelterless fields to the school when it opened in June. June was the month of rain and lightning. This school was owned by Kelan, an untouchable, but one who had not forgotten his lowly birth; he had come to Sivaraman Nair and sought his blessing.

'Prosper, O untouchable!' the feudal chief had said—that was a long time ago and he had meant do not prosper beyond limits. But Kelan had prospered. Kelan's wife had come dressed in shining sarees and made offerings to the little gods of Khasak. Kalyanikutti had watched her, a sad spinster trapped inside her feudal home. Kelan's school and his burgeoning property began to aggravate Sivaraman Nair; he denounced all teaching by the low-born, he talked ramblingly to the villagers and even more to himself. He was ill. The doctors in Palghat town strapped a pneumatic tube round his arm, took readings and put him under sedation . . . . When the new school came to Khasak, Sivaraman Nair felt revived. It was to be on his property, and would make a better school. He had offered his seedling house to the District Board. The seedling house would henceforth be the school, and nobody's rendezvous.

'Where will you store the seedlings?' Narayani had asked in scarcely disguised anger.

'Damn the seedlings!' Sivaraman Nair had said in reply.

It was the night after the disastrous panchayat meeting; the mullah sat in his tiny strip of verandah trying to mend his broken sandal. Thithi Bi watched her husband's labour, the frayed leather and the kitchen knife. She said, 'The Sheikh will not forsake us.' The mullah punched and stitched futilely. She had given him money to mend the sandal; instead, he had bought her a copper ring embossed with a piece of honed glass.

'Why didn't you get the sandal mended?'

She stretched her hand into the tiny halo of the kerosene wick and stuck out the finger with the ring on. Allah-Pitcha turned towards her and smiled, and resumed the mending. 'Great King of the Universe,' she said, 'protect us!'

Promises weren't kept; many children joined the school, even the grandchildren of the red-bearded conservatives. A day more for the school to open. The last namaz was over; the congregation had consisted of just two old men. The mullah sat alone in the mosque a long while. The priest and his flock, and even this house of worship were passing through trying times; the mullah stroked his beard, a mere frazzle of silver and brown, as he did whenever he contemplated his own dissolution. From the mosque the mullah could see the school far away. Ravi's bedside lamp burned bright, the schoolmaster was perhaps reading, as the learned do, to fall asleep. The mullah hadn't seen him face to face. The women of the village said he was young and handsome. For a moment Allah-Pitcha contemplated visiting him, talking to him, but lost his nerve; what was he but an unlettered priest? From the school the mullah's gaze turned towards Chetali. Beyond the mountain lay untrodden tracks. Great unseen rains fell on those timeless springheads and the waters avalanched down muddy and turbulent, leaving the silt of age on the enfeebled pilgrim.

The mullah stepped out of the mosque, leaning on his stick. His way home lay past the school. He crossed the yard and paused awhile at the gate of the mosque. He thought of the stranger in the seedling house with sympathy and love. Innocent wayfarer, what bond of karma brings you here?

Then the lamp in the seedling house went out.

Once Upon A Time

IT WAS THE first day of school and Ravi was standing beside the blackboard. Like the mullah he wondered too: What karmic bond has brought me here? What purpose, what meticulous pre-determination? Then came a gust of wind which threw open the window behind him. Ravi went to the window and stood looking out. The children left their seats and crowded round him to look through the window and see the beautiful thing their village had framed for their teacher.

It was the lotus pond of Khasak, proud in newly blooming purple.

'Hey,' said Ravi, 'there is a little bird caught in the lotus meshes!'

'A chick of the waterfowl, Saar!' the children said, and looked up at their teacher. Did he share their excitement?

'Waterfowl?' asked Ravi. 'Then it won't drown.'

'It might if it tires, Saar.'

'Shall we pull it out?' Ravi asked the class.

A dozen voices chimed together, 'Let us!'

'Wait a minute,' Ravi said, 'there are two more birds now . . . .'

'It's Attha and Umma.'

The parent birds pecked away the meshes. Soon the

chick, its parents on either side, was waddling ceremoniously along the bank.

It was a sunny day. Tiny wind-blown clouds floated by, their shadows moved like cows grazing over the pastures of Khasak. Ravi came back to his seat and called the class to order. He sat long in silence, sharing the memory of that framed vision with his twenty pupils who sat before him like postulants.

'Maash!'

It was Madhavan Nair calling from the gate.

'Can we interrupt the lessons?'

'Welcome,' said Ravi, 'the school is yours.'

Madhavan Nair came in with two unkempt children in tow. He had been busy till the previous night, trying to persuade parents to send their children to the school.

'Have you anything against savages?' Madhavan Nair asked.

The two boys stood bewildered, their slight figures lost in immense thatches of hair and shirts as roomy as surplices.

'Two more for your rolls,' Madhavan Nair said. 'Sons of basket weavers from the mountains. They tried to run away but I caught them and made them promise they would enroll. Hey, you!'

One of them had a running nose and was trying to breathe in the snot.

'Blow your nose, you unclean one,' Madhavan Nair admonished.

Ravi patted the child, and said encouragingly, 'Don't worry. The well is over there, draw some water and wash.'

The little savage bounded off and was back in a trice.

'*Ayyo!*' Madhavan Nair cried out. 'This is catastrophe . . . .' The child had washed his face first and then blown his nose, and now his shirt front was soiled.

Ravi saw the mess on the shirt and the beatific smile.

'The shirt!' the tailor lamented. 'It's ruined!'

The fabric, not yet laundered, had the glaze of calendering, and would not absorb the water.

'There goes my time and money,' the tailor went on. 'I made these shirts roomy enough for them to grow up in.'

'That's a good boy,' Ravi coaxed, 'Shall I write down your name in this big book?'

'Write them down, Maash!' Madhavan Nair said. 'This is Chatthan and this, Perakkadan, inseparables like Rama and Lakshmana. And if they stop coming to school, I'll tear these shirts off their backs.'

Ravi wrote the names down in the register, and turned to the tailor, 'You have all helped so much . . . .'

Madhavan Nair grew bashful and pretended not to hear the compliment; he stepped into the little aisle between the benches and began cheering the children as one would a football team. 'Alam Khan!' he called out, 'Kunhamina, my beauty!' he chucked her under the chin, 'and goodness gracious, who's this but Kholusu . . . .' The class stirred in pleasant disorder. Madhavan Nair could well have taken over, but he chose to conclude the encounter with a little advice, 'See this Master-Etta here. He has passed the fourteenth standard. You children should study like him and become engineers. You will, won't you?'

The children chorused, 'We will!'

Madhavan Nair left, and Ravi was alone with the class again; he opened the register and silently read the names. Then he reread them, names of caliphs and queens, indigent dynasties which had strayed out of desert sanctuaries and become marooned in Khasak.

The day warmed, the palm winds were blowing. It was the hour of the teacher. Ravi smiled upon his twenty-two children, and they smiled back, the caliphs and queens, until smiles filled the seedling house. This was the hour of myth, Ravi knew. 'Let's tell a story,' he said to the children. They were overjoyed.

Ravi asked, 'What kind of story?'

The children began chirping all together, and a ten-year-old in the front row raised her hand to tell him something. Her silver anklets chimed when she moved her feet under the desk, and her wide gaze was hemmed by exuberant lashes darkened with surma.

'Yes?' Ravi said.

'Saar, Saar . . .' she said, then grew shy.

'A story without dying, Saar!'

Ravi laughed, 'What's your name, child?'

'Kunhamina.'

Ravi listened to the ballad of Khasak in her, its heroic periods, its torrential winds and its banyan breezes. There was no death but only silver anklets and her eyes sparkling through the surma. Ravi looked deep into those eyes; the story would have no dying, only the slow and mysterious transit. He began in the style of the ancient fabulist.

'Once upon a time . . . .'

Ravi's days went by in order and peace. Madhavan Nair had brought him a maid to sweep and swab and cook a frugal meal that would last the day. Abida was the daughter of Chukkru the diver from an earlier marriage. Her mother was found dead in one of the village wells. Some said Chukkru had drowned her, others believed it was the work of a jealous lover. Abida was a child when it happened. After the days of mourning, Chukkru ranged again through far-flung places to return home at the dead of night. Little Abida grew up crying. A wet glaze lay over her eyes, an orphan glaze, as though the tears hadn't dried in them.

On days when there was no school, Abida stayed longer, tidying up the old seedling house as best as she could.

On Sunday Ravi became aware of the pallor on her face. He asked, 'Not well, Abida?'

'I'm well, Saar. It's a mild fever which comes on sometimes.'

'You ought to see a doctor, a vaidyan.'

She replied disinterestedly, 'I suppose so.'

On another Sunday, watching her bend and sway at work, Ravi realized how short she was, and how slight.

'Are you fifteen,' Ravi guessed at her age, 'or younger?'

'Twenty,' she said, her face sad as she answered him.

'Abida, can you read and write?'

'No.'

'Listen, Abida . . . .'

'Yes, Saar?'

'I'm going to put you to school.'

She was on her knees, cleaning up a crevice on the floor. She rose, arms akimbo, and laughed.

'Me, Saar?'

'Yes. You could find yourself a job in Palghat, say, in a nursing home . . . .'

She didn't laugh now, but looked at him through her undried childhood tears. 'I shouldn't leave this village,' she said. 'If I do, there'll be nobody to look after Attha.'

'His wife . . .' Ravi began, and fell silent. Morosely Abida resumed her work. Attha had a beautiful wife, but he lived and died in loneliness, wandering from well to well, retrieving things fallen into the dormant slime. He had none save her, the child he had brought up in a well of loneliness.

But she had her people, in a manner of speaking, an uncle and her maternal grandmother in the faraway village of Kalikavu. The ancestral home on a hill was now in ruins, lines of mouldering brick sinking into the earth. Within these bounds stood a hut of mud and thatch in which the grandmother and uncle lived. The grandmother was blind and the uncle leprous. Sometimes, on a cloudless evening, the villagers below would catch sight of him, seated among the ruins, his stiff, flat palms held out to take the sun.

Ravi sat on his cot, leaning on a stack of pillows, and looked out of the window. The sun was setting. The grazing herd of clouds was gone. Soon it was dark, and the fantasy returned, the fantasy of the journey. The seedling house became a compartment in a train, and he the lone and imprisoned traveller. Dark wastes lay on either side; from them fleeting signs spoke to Ravi—a solitary firefly, a plodding lantern. The wheels moved along the track with soft, deceptive thuds. Then he heard the far rush of another track racing towards his own, the sorrow of another futilely seeking comfort. The rails met for one moment, tumultuously, to part again. To race away into the many mysteried night.

Uneasy Neighbours

HAVING SPENT ITSELF in the first blinding onrush, the monsoon lay over Khasak, indrawn, in samadhi.

The single-teacher school was now three months old, its strength an unstable twenty. The children came like moving huts, sharing the shelter of large handleless palm-frond umbrellas, heedless of time, as they stopped to play in the rain streams; they lingered at the school gate, some came in, while some turned away splashing and screaming, chasing the creatures of the rain. Helplessly Ravi watched the palm-frond thatches stray back into illiteracy. Some of them never came back, but there were unexpected entrants who came to watch the King's angular alphabet being written out on the blackboard. Sometimes an earlier escapee returned to nostalgic reunion.

Ravi was calling the rolls one morning. When he came to the name of Hyder Hazrat, it was an unfamiliar voice that answered. Ravi looked up.

'Who's that?'

The newcomer stood up.

'You aren't Hyder Hazrat.'

'No, Saar.'

'Then?'

'He lent me his slate and pencil, Saar.'

'Very well. Your name?'

The boy continued standing and smiling but wouldn't speak. The other children coaxed him, 'Tell Saar your name, you clumsy one.'

'Karuvu,' the boy said. It was a name from a long lost dialect.

'Sounds beautiful,' Ravi said.

The class was astir. All of them talking together, they told Ravi that it was a name given to boys of the Thottiya caste; the Thottiyas were an ancient martial clan, but now they roamed the villages with their performing monkeys to make a living.

Ten-year-old Karuvu did not quite relish this introduction, but neither was he unduly resentful. He stood smiling.

'Well, Karuvu,' Ravi said, 'now go and blow your nose outside, and come back.'

'Do what Saar tells you,' little Sohra prodded.

When Karuvu came back, Ravi made him stand near the table.

'You like the school,' Ravi said, 'don't you?'

Karuvu smiled on.

'Since you don't dislike it,' Ravi continued, 'let's say you'll like it tomorrow and the day after . . . .'

'He will, Saar!' the children said in chorus.

Ravi pulled out the admissions register.

'Your father's name?'

'Chenthiyavu Thottiya, monkey-trainer.'

'Interesting,' Ravi said, and for want of a better conversational opening, he asked, 'How many monkeys does you father have?'

'Sixteen.'

'A lie, Saar!' said Kunhamina. 'He is boasting, Saar! His father has only two monkeys.'

'One makes mistakes while counting,' Ravi said. 'Now I shall enter your name in this big book.'

Ravi wrote: *C. Karuvu, son of Mr Chenthiyavu Thottiya, prominent monkey-trainer.*

Meanwhile, the basket-weavers had made a few ominous visits to the school. On their last visit they had told Ravi that he should free their children from the oath the tailor had extracted under duress.

Ravi was puzzled; after much persuasion the wild visitors deigned to let him into the clan's secret. Their language had no script, as only a scriptless language could help them penetrate the forest depths. Chatthan and Perakkadan spent restless days at school, presenting themselves as their oath to the mountain gods required of them, but keeping away from letters in palpable horror. Finally, the inevitable happened. Ravi and Madhavan Nair looked on helplessly as the boys were led away in their yet unwashed surplices.

Madhavan Nair had spread the word that Ravi was a Bachelor of Arts. 'Impossible!' commented the mullah when he heard it. With a bachelor's degree one could get bigger, better jobs. In the meantime Aliyar made a discovery. On weekends he went to Palghat town to replenish his stocks and buy old newspapers from the garbage dealer. Paper to pack the vadas in, Aliyar would say, though few believed him, because invariably the papers were ones that carried pictures of women in scanty clothing. Once when Ravi was passing by the teashop Aliyar had called him in, 'Maeshtar, could you tell us what is in this newspaper?'

Ravi stepped in and took the paper from Aliyar and glanced through it.

'This woman with nothing on, what is it all about?'

Ravi handed back the paper, it was an old German tabloid.

'I can't read this,' he said.

The conversation froze.

Later, Aliyar sent for Appa Mutthu, the most educated young man in Khasak, one who had failed in the eighth standard in Kelan's school.

'Read it, O child of Satan!' Aliyar said.

Appa Mutthu brightened at the sight of the pin-up, and read with noisy confidence, 'Ell . . . Cee . . . Peeee . . . .' He read on with great seriousness, as if he were breaking a cryptogram. His audience wanted to know more, they asked him where it was that women went about stripped. Appa Mutthu concentrated.

'Ooo . . . Eee . . . hey, there is something wrong here, there is an upside down V over this O , and this E sports a tuft . . . .'

'Tell us about the woman.'

What kind of Bachelor of Arts was this, who couldn't read what Appa Mutthu could? The story of Ravi being a doctor's son too must be a lie. It was Madhavan Nair who had told them that Ravi's father was a doctor in a big plantation. 'A lie!' said the mullah. It was simple reasoning that a young man with that kind of parentage wouldn't teach in a village school.

'Please, let us grant there could be some truth in all this,' said a voice from outside. The gossip-bird, Kuppu-Acchan, perched on the load-rest, had been listening.

'Truth?' the mullah said, 'It is a fraud!'

'Maybe he is the son of a lesser kind of doctor, a homavathi perhaps.'

A homavathi, Khasak's slang for a homeopath, was held in contempt because he dispensed sugar pellets for all ailments.

'A confidence trick,' the mullah said.

It was dark. The mullah put down his lantern on the culvert wall where the pathway forked. He stood there, his mind vacant. Madhavan Nair, passing that way, tapped him awake.

'What foolish plan now?' he taunted the priest.

'None.'

Madhavan Nair looked at the mullah's shirt, a patchwork of yarn that had decayed with age. He felt sorry for him and said, 'Stop playing games.'

The mullah protested feebly and stuttered, 'What . . . what have I done?'

'Nothing,' said the tailor, 'it is Kelan who's doing it. For every child you stop from the Board's school Kelan pays you a bribe. If you stop a sufficient number our school will close. Who will bribe you then?'

Madhavan Nair let go of the mullah's arm and walked away towards the fields. The mullah saw the light in the school window. On most evenings he passed by that light. He did so today as well. Wearily, he turned towards the village square . . . .

Maimoona had converted her verandah into a little shop where she sold odds and ends of grocery. The mullah saw her seated in the light of a pendent lamp. Pretty as a malic, an angel, he thought as he blessed her silently . . . . He came and sat down on the bench laid out in front of the shop. Maimoona did not look up.

'Maimoo,' he enquired, 'hasn't Chukkru got back yet?'

'No,' she answered curtly.

'Is the pain in your hips any better?'

'Mmm.'

The mullah lingered on, unable to make conversation.

He watched a few fragile moths fly and burn their wings on the pendent lamp.

'Maimoo, my child,' he said after a difficult silence, 'can you give me a quart of coconut oil? I shall pay you soon.'

'There isn't any oil to spare.'

'Your Umma's hair has become dry . . . .'

'Go away, Attha!'

'Well,' the mullah spoke in an even feebler voice, 'then I shan't trouble you. Look after your hip pain, take some herbal potion.'

The mullah rose, took another sullen round of the village and walked back towards the school. Ravi saw the wandering light, the magic lantern moving towards the school . . . . The mullah coughed to make Ravi aware of his presence.

'Come in,' Ravi said. The mullah stepped in hesitantly.

'What a pleasant surprise!' Ravi said.

'*Assalam Aleikum*!'

'*Waleikum Salaam*. The great mullah of Khasak is ignoring his guests.'

The mullah, slowly and with much effort, folded himself to sit cross-legged on the floor at the foot of the cot on which Ravi was resting.

'Sit up on the cot, Mollaka.'

'I'm comfortable here, Kutti.'

The mullah put out the lantern to save kerosene.

'What are you reading, Kutti? Is it a Veda?'

'Oh, no! This is just a story.'

'What class has one to study to understand this book?'

Ravi laughed, 'Well . . . .'

'Is it in English?'

'Yes.'

For a moment the priest withdrew into himself to make an entry in a dark book of memories.

'Have a cigarette, Mollakka.'

'No, Kutti. I have a bidi. Cigarettes do not suit my throat. Or, well, I might as well smoke the cigarette as you offer it in friendship.'

The mullah held the cigarette between thumb and forefinger and burned it out in avid pulls.

'I have come to talk about a certain matter,' the mullah said, 'and it is in your hands.'

'I'll be happy if I can be of any help . . . .'

'I heard you were looking for a low paid maintenance person, a masalji.'

'Oh, yes. I need one to sweep and swab the school. It's too much for Abida, so I decided she'd just do the cooking. The District Board will pay five rupees a month, it isn't much. Know anyone who could do the job?'

'I . . . I will do it.'

The mullah's voice was hardly audible, and Ravi was embarrassed. The job was looked upon with a certain disfavour. Not quite knowing what to say, Ravi said, 'As you wish, Mollakka.'

'Now I will take leave.'

The mullah rose. He took one stick from Ravi's box of matches and lit his lantern.

The First Lessons

THE RAINS WERE over, the skies shone, and Khasak readied itself for Onam, the festival of thanksgiving. Children went up into the hills at sunrise to gather flowers. For ten days they would arrange colourful designs in their yards with flower petals to welcome the deities of the festival. Ravi heard the children sing on the hillsides, and for a fleeting moment they touched him with the joy of a hundred home-comings. The moment passed, and once again he was the fugitive. A fugitive had no home, no Sarai, no festival.

Ravi sought to share his fears with Madhavan Nair—the Onam recess would last a fortnight. Would the children come back to dreary routine after that spell of freedom?

'If I were their age, I wouldn't !' Ravi said.

'You lost your childhood somewhere along the way, Maash. I hope the children find it for you.'

As they parted Madhavan Nair said with some hesitation, 'There is one more pupil for you if you can take a risk.'

'A risk? Who's it anyway?'

Guilt and remorse made Madhavan Nair suggest it to

Ravi. Some days ago Appu-Kili's mother Neeli had been at his shop waiting for him to put the finishing stitches to a blouse he was making for her. She sat there bare-breasted, watching the dressmaker anticipate the contours.

'There, there!' she had said suddenly. 'See, O Venerable Nair . . . .'

On the other side of the square there were children at play. In their midst stood the cretin, taller than them and clad in conspicuous motley. Madhavan Nair remembered how she had broken down as she pointed to Appu-Kili and said, 'Look at my son!'

It was just the other day that Madhavan Nair had made him that weird toga with scraps of cloth. He had scissored out a Gandhi and a sickle-and-hammer from discarded gunny bags, and stitched them on either side of the toga.

'If only you could tell the Maeshtar . . . .' Neeli had sobbed.

Madhavan Nair had seen the tears fall on her bare breasts.

'I shall speak to him, Neeli.'

'Not to teach him, but to stop him from roaming with children.'

When the school reopened after the festival break, Ravi was pleasantly surprised to find the school had survived the vacation . . . . Madhavan Nair arrived chaperoning Appu-Kili. The children crowded round the cretin who was neither man nor child. Ravi herded them back to their seats, taking care the dragonfly, his cretin's constant comparison, was not lost. He drew the Parrot aside and asked him gently, 'Like to join the school, Kili?'

Madhavan Nair raised his hand to discipline the

children, 'Quieten down, evil ones! You are upsetting my Parrot!' And to Kili, 'Didn't you hear what the Maash-Etta asked you? Speak, O Parrot of the Palms!'

Appu-Kili stood looking indifferent, his gaze on his toes.

'Why are you afraid?' Madhavan Nair reasoned. 'Isn't it our own school?'

That did not reassure the Parrot. The children in the school were all his playmates, they made signs of encouragement. From the benches came hushed invitations: Come, Kili, come here, sit near me! As Madhavan Nair turned to go, Appu-Kili let out a howl, 'Take me with you, Madhavan-Etto!'

'O avian!' the tailor despaired, 'you have put me to shame!'

Madhavan Nair took four coppers from his purse and asked one of the pupils, Alam Khan, to go and get some murukkus. He told Kili that the teacher would give him the murukkus if he sat quietly and did his lessons. Appu-Kili cheered up.

Ravi whispered, 'Madhavan Nair, my life is in peril. This prehistoric pet of yours . . . .

'Have no fear, Maash.'

Ravi found the child-man a place next to little Sohra.

'Sohra will take care of you, my winged being!' Madhavan Nair said, and added this parting advice. 'Study well, and become an engineer.'

'He will!' the class responded.

As Ravi turned to write out a sum on the blackboard, Sohra drew the Kili close and passed him a sweet berry.

'Don't be afraid, Kili, I'm with you.'

During the Onam vacation cobwebs had gathered in the

seedling house, and Ravi set apart a day for teacher and pupils to clean up the school. It became a war on the spiders. Adam drew a line on the floor with chalk and laid out the dead spiders. Appu-Kili picked up the biggest of them and tried to breathe life into it.

'Saar, Saar,' Kunhamina asked, 'how big are the really big spiders?'

Ravi pointed to the dome of the mosque, and said, 'That big.'

'*Yaa Rahman*!'

The spiders in the crevices of the walls were brown, and were only as big as an outspread palm. But outside, in the forests of the rain, they were born to power and splendour. Like the kings of old they revelled in the hunt. And in the teeming nights of fear they rose like stars of the nether dark . . . . Ravi told the children the story of the spiders, how after they made love the female ate up her mate. The children could not believe that such bloody dynasties ruled over Khasak's peaceful grass and fern. Then Karuvu stood up and said the male spider was paying for his sins in an earlier birth. The children knew it was karma, the class was now unusually quiet.

The story of karma ended, but Ravi had set the children on a magic trail. They refused to do sums and recitations, and for the next two days Ravi did nothing but tell them stories of plants and animals. It was during one of these heady lessons that Kunhamina brought a hedge lizard to the classroom. The lizard made no attempt to escape.

'Hurt it, have you?' Ravi asked Kunhamina.

'No, Saar. Just doped it with castor sap.'

The lizard took a few unsteady steps on Ravi's table, then gave up, and looked around in ancient derision.

Kunhamina had reckoned that Ravi would be pleased with the catch, but froze when she sensed his displeasure.

'Will it die?' Ravi asked Kunhamina. She wouldn't answer, but the rest of the class spoke. The castor sap, said Madhavi, was like the liquor they made in Khasak, it killed only when one had too much of it. Adam said hedge lizards were used in sorcery, he terrified himself with the thought of saturnine deities called up by the sorcerer. No child of Khasak was friends with the hedge lizard said Karuvu, because it sucked the blood of children, sucked it through the air from afar. One realized it only when one watched the lizard's head suddenly turn crimson, the sign of the vampire.

There was more about the hedge lizard—the evil spirits exorcised by the astrologers went into exile riding the hedge lizard. They wouldn't say anything more as it was Khasak's secret.

Ravi and the children were engrossed in the stories and no one had noticed Kunhamina sobbing.

'Kunhamina,' Ravi said, 'I didn't mean to hurt you.'

That only made the sobbing worse. Tears brought the surma down in patches over her cheeks, and the silver anklets chimed as she moved her legs disconsolately beneath her desk. In the meantime the lizard recovered, and with one last look at everyone, stalked out of the classroom towards the hedges. Kunhamina smiled.

That day Ravi told the children the story of the lizards. In times before Man usurped the earth, the lizard held sway. A miraculous book opened, the children saw its pages rise and turn and flop. Out of it came mighty saurians moving slowly in deep canyons after the dull scent of prey, and pterodactyls rose screaming over their nesting precipices.

The story was reluctantly interrupted for lunch; after hurried morsels the children raced back to school and huddled round their teacher. The pages rose and fell again . . . . Long before the lizards, before the dinosaurs, two spores set out on an incredible journey. They came to a valley bathed in the placid glow of sunset.

My elder sister, said the little spore to the bigger spore, let us see what lies beyond.

This valley is green, replied the bigger spore, I shall journey no farther.

I want to journey, said the little spore, I want to discover. She gazed in wonder at the path before her.

Will you forget your sister, asked the bigger spore.

Never, said the little spore.

You will, little one, for this is the loveless tale of karma; in it there is only parting and sorrow.

The little spore journeyed on. The bigger spore stayed back in the valley. Her roots pierced the damp earth and sought the nutrients of death and memory. She sprouted over the earth, green and contented . . . . A girl with silver anklets and eyes prettied with surma came to Chetali's valley to gather flowers. The Champaka tree stood alone—efflorescent, serene. The flower-gatherer reached out and held down a soft twig to pluck the flowers. As the twig broke the Champaka said, My little sister, you have forgotten me!

The children had gone home. Ravi closed his eyes, leaned back in his chair and abandoned himself to the old weariness. Around him rose the scent of incense, and the sound of bells and cymbals.

Vedan Uddharate Jagannivahate—the sloka celebrating the avatars of the Lord, evolute incarnations from fish to boar to man and deity resounded over everything.

The moment passed. Ravi, now awake, looked out. The sun was setting over Chetali's valley. The sunset filled the seedling house with the warmth of a sensuous fever.

The Well Within

CHUKKRU WAS FIFTY when he married Maimoona. He looked only sixty, commented Kuppu-Acchan viciously . . . .

Chukkru followed an unusual calling. He dived and retrieved things fallen into wells. A pulley or a battered bucket, a pitcher of copper or bronze, at times a gold or silver ornament. Often there was nothing to be retrieved, but he wandered from well to well and from village to village, over desolate paths and distances. Those were times before there was piped water, and there were wells in almost every house—the more prosperous the family the deeper the well. Chukkru ranged over the Palghat countryside, by now familiar with the cry of his calling—a long, sad drone in which pots and pans lay lost as in the slime of wells. They called him the Diving Fowl.

In the years of perilous diving, Chukkru's name atrophied, he became a diving fowl; Kuppu-Acchan said that the fowl would peck grains of rice if one were to throw a fistful in his path.

When the marriage was fixed the villagers said it would never really take place and if at all it did, the bride wouldn't stay long. But these fond expectations were belied. Maimoona walked unperturbed into wedlock.

There was no honeymoon; the Diving Fowl left Khasak before dawn the day after and came home after midnight, covered with leeches and moss. Maimoona picked his skin clean and put him to sleep across her navel. She woke up to her days as usual and walked across the square, the thattan slipping from her hair, sleeves rolled up in grand display.

She turned the front of the Diving Fowl's hut into a shop, more for gossip and amusement than for material gain; she spent hours there with her friend and confidante, Thanka the jaggery-seller . . . . Abida had grown up watching Maimoona from a distance, and like most girls her age, was stricken by a strange love for her beauty. But when Maimoona moved into their house, Abida felt a greater loneliness than before. It was hard for her to consider the newcomer as a stepmother; Maimoona was just seven years older. But couldn't call her 'elder sister' either.

Abida had always been lonely. This girl, timid and apprehensive, sorrow hidden in the pallor of her cheeks, had found no playmate while a child and no young man when she came of age. When the wind had taken away the heat of sunlight, she would wander along the big ridge across the paddies, or sit by the lotus pond watching the water birds. Often Thitthi Bi would ask her, 'Have you no friend, my child?' and Abida would reply, 'None, Umma.' And Thitthi Bi would bless her, 'The holy Sheikh be your companion!'

But there was someone to love, someone to serve and care for—her Attha. She would warm the gruel around midnight and wait for Attha. Now it was Maimoona who warmed the gruel, and on many nights Attha went to bed without seeing his daughter. Yet Abida stayed awake in her corridor until Maimoona's crooning gave way to the fitful snores of her Attha.

Abida would attempt an overture at times, tentative and ingratiating, 'Tell me a story.'

'The story of your mother's lover,' Maimoona would ask, 'the one who killed her?'

It was on such occasions that Abida slipped out of the house without catching anyone's attention, gliding like a spirit. Once she escaped and went into the grove of Arasu trees. She sat down beneath a tree and asked, 'Holy Sheikh, are you with me?' Suddenly the brook turned a deeper blue, and there was a rain of flowers.

'*Yah Rahman*,' she said. Her inward ear listened intently. In that ecstasy she became a child once again. She heard the horse's trot in the wind.

'Horse-spirit, horse-spirit,' she said, 'will you give me a ride across the sky?' She mounted the horse-spirit, and together they raced in the wind, past forests and over seas. Then she saw her mother. She stood young and radiant once more, but at Abida's touch, she began to shrivel and moulder. Abida found herself in the doomed house on the hill. Outside, her uncle sat on a rock holding up his palms to the warmth of the setting sun.

'Horse-spirit, horse-spirit!' Abida called out. She could hear the hooves no more, she was alone beneath the tree. The east wind blew in giant sighs through the grove of Arasus.

'Maimoona,' Allah-Pitcha once reasoned with his daughter, 'I don't think it is wise to send Abida out as a servant. She's no longer a girl.'

'Who's sending her?' Maimoona taunted, 'She likes to flirt around.'

The next day Abida did not go to school. As the day grew warmer, Thanka the jaggery woman came to laze about and gossip. Abida could hear them whisper and giggle.

'Who's there in the corridor?' Maimoona asked, leaning back and speaking into the window.

'It's me,' Abida responded.

'Didn't you go to sweep the school?'

No reply came from Abida.

'Aren't you going?'

Still Abida was silent.

'You had better go,' Maimoona said. 'Do you expect the Diving Fowl to fly home with your food?'

It was Sunday. Quietly, Abida slipped out and took the footway towards the seedling house. She found Ravi, broom in hand, sweeping. Quickly she seized the broom.

'Not you, Saar!' she said.

'True,' Ravi laughed, 'I can't sweep half as well . . . .

'*Yaa Allah!*' she said. It was that day, without her realizing how, that she told him her story.

'You are not alone, Abida,' Ravi said, 'I too am a motherless child.'

'*Rabbil Aalemeen!*'

Abida stooped to sweep. Ravi was standing close. 'Abida,' he said to her.

'Yes, Saar?'

'You don't look too well.'

He laid a caring hand over her forehead.

'You have a fever, my little girl.'

She smiled in gratitude. 'Ah, yes,' she said, 'it keeps coming and going.'

'Go home and lie down.'

As she walked home she wept without restraint. Suddenly she stopped; it was no good going home in that state. She turned towards the brook to wash her face and cool her feet. Appu-Kili was there, stalking the big green dragonflies. He was overjoyed to see her.

'Came to see me?'

'Of course, what else would I come here for, my Parrot?'

Strangely, Abida realized that she had spoken the truth and touched a mysterious springhead of solace.

Meanwhile Appu-Kili had caught a dragonfly and with nimble fingers slipped a lasso round its tail. Abida looked at the dragonfly, into its eyes of a thousand crystals. The eyes shone dully with the chronicles of the dead. If dragonflies were memories of the dead, as they believed in Khasak, whose then was this memory? Perhaps it was her mother's pining images of sin and regret and drowning. The crystal eyes fell on her.

'My Parrot,' Abida said, 'why do you hold the ancient one in your lasso? Let him go his way.'

Appu-Kili began to cry. Quickly she said, 'I'm sorry. I didn't mean it.'

The tears stopped, the cretin's smile spread over his face, big and beatific. 'No ask me leave him?'

'Oh no!'

Appu-Kili undid a cloth wrap and laid it before her, 'Take it.' Champaka flowers. She folded her thattan and gathered the flowers in it. She walked home with a Champaka in each of her earrings, and placed the thattan filled with flowers before Maimoona.

Thanka was still there, whispering and giggling. Maimoona took the flowers, adorned her earrings with them, and gave generous fistfuls to Thanka. Abida walked away into her dingy corridor. Maimoona said, within Abida's hearing, 'Wearing flowers, that bag of bones!'

Abida bore the venom of those words. She tried to soothe it with a prayer. She took up the broom and tried to sweep the corridor, but couldn't. She leant the broom against the wall. There was a bowl of souring gruel, she took a spoonful, but it tasted foul and she did not eat any more.

Abida walked out again. Maimoona did not ask her where she was going. Abida went back to the grove of Arasus. The place was deserted. In the enchantment of the grove she became a dragonfly; whose memory was she? Perhaps a memory of her own sorrows of another birth. From the grove she walked to the brook, she plucked the two Champakas from her ears and tore the petals into fragments and gently dropped them into the water.

Appu-Kili was still amid the screw pines. He saw Abida drop the petals into the water, and was saddened.

'Achchi, he said, 'what you doing with fovers?'

'O my Parrot, I was playing.'

He came over and stood near her. 'You aa bootiful,' he said, soothingly. 'I marry you. You like?'

'Of course, my Parrot.'

'Get you more flowers.'

Appu-Kili went back to the screw pines. Again, Abida was alone beside the brook. She sat down on the soft carpet of Krishna Kantis, the blue-flowered grass. The brook flowed on with the remnants of many things.

The village said that Maimoona was becoming more beautiful. She walked through Khasak as she always had, she sat in her shop for long hours with Thanka.

One day Abida came and stood before them. She was no longer afraid. She said, 'Let Attha come home. I'll tell him.'

For a brief moment Maimoona went pale, but soon she was her normal self.

Pouting, she said. 'What are you going to tell?'

'That the Khazi comes here . . . .'

Thanka was the one who flared up, 'Ah ha! Can't the Khazi come here to ward off spirits?'

'I'll tell . . . .'

'Let's see you do that, little slut!' Thanka said in a tearing rage. Then to Maimoona, 'Nip this in the bud . . . .'

'Thanka, it's nothing . . . .' Maimoona said.

At midnight Khasak woke up to screams and the sounds of a chase; Abida was running towards the mullah's house, blood flowing from the gash in her forehead, with Chukkru, brandishing a log of firewood, in hot pursuit.

Quickly Thitthi Bi took the girl in and closed the door.

'What has come over you, old sinner?' Thitthi Bi barred his way.

The Diving Fowl gasped for breath in anger and exhaustion.

'Open the door, Thitthi Bi-Akka,' he panted, 'bring her out!'

Chukkru stood in the yard, incensed.

Now the mullah stepped down into the yard, drew his knife out of its scabbard in the broad canvas belt, and held it up.

'Take this,' the mullah said, 'and this too,' he said touching his head with the knife, 'it's greyed, cut it off, and then have your way.'

The Diving Fowl threw away the log of firewood and walked home downcast. The mullah went to the closed door and said, 'Abida, my child, don't go back, sleep here.'

The next morning the houri walked again, fresh roses in her earrings . . . . Abida slept the whole day, and got up at sundown.

'Umma,' Abida said, 'Let me go up to the brook. I'll feel better after a dip.'

The fading sunlight was turning crimson. Abida recalled the many remnants of things the stream contained, she remembered the froth and eddy of the water as it bore them away. She crossed the brook and began her walk over the ridge. Far beyond Khasak, she saw the train race towards the mountain pass like a serpent with a flaming jewel on its forehead. Now the black palmyras were lost in the oncoming night. The village of Kalikavu was far away.

Many miles from Khasak, in that red and darkening twilight, the Diving Fowl perched on the wall round a well. The well was ancient, bounded on all sides by the four wings of the old manor. The Diving Fowl sat there and contemplated the plunge. Deep down lay the water, luminous in the dark, like a diviner's crystal. There was a song he had composed years ago, a lullaby for the motherless Abida. As he divined the gleaming ripples below, the song came back to him. From his perch, Chukkru sang it in his rusted and dissonant voice:

> *'O my old fish*
> *With the fat old head!*
> *Bring my crying daughter*
> *A big glowing pearl.'*

He dived into the well, and deeper, into the well within the well. The water was like many crystal doors and silken curtains. Chukkru made his way past crystal and silk, and moved towards the mystery that had lured him all his life—the sacred dark! As Chukkru journeyed on, the last of the crystal doors closed behind him.

The Tiger

THE KHAZI STOOD over Chukkru's grave and stomped on its sodden cover; he stood in the desolate graveyard and listened to the secret noontide noises. Then he turned and walked out over the ridge towards the hut that stood on a patch of chalkstone and brittle grass. He paused at the gate and called out, 'Anyone in?'

This was the hut Neeli shared with her four sisters and their husbands. The men were tree-fellers who were often away for days together. The wives worked in the fields of Khasak.

Neeli stayed back to keep house, while the only other inmate, Appu-Kili, was at school, or off on his moody wanderings.

Neeli peeped out at the caller. The Khazi raised a hand and spoke in the sonorous tone of the dervish, 'The blessings of the Sheikh I bring hither!'

Neeli mumbled a welcome which was lost in a flow of sibilants. The Khazi came in and sat down on the mat Neeli had spread for him on the floor.

'Your son?' the Khazi enquired with a measure of anxiety.

'At school, O Khazi. Studying!'

'Good tidings!'

'My son . . .' she sobbed as the delusion of his schooling disintegrated into stark reality.

'Your son is possessed. Within him dwell great demons, poothams.'

'Truly, O Khazi?'

'And you too are possessed.'

Neeli leaned against the wall, dismayed.

'Have no fear,' the Khazi said, 'I shall lure them out with spells and banish them for ever!'

It was in this solitary hut that Appu-Kili was born twenty years ago, the child of five mothers. Nachi, Kochi, Pechi, Kali and Neeli were sisters. The first four had married, but brought forth no children. Neeli, who had no husband, delivered when she was sixteen. The three older brothers-in-law wanted her out, but Kuttappu, Kali's husband, said that mother and child would stay, and since he was given to much violence, the rest of them gave in. Mother and child stayed. The child bore a striking resemblance to Kuttappu, which Kali and Neeli said was perhaps due to the name they had given him—Appu was one half of Kuttappu. Soon the four barren women overcame their embarrassment and built gorgeous fantasies of motherhood around little Appu. When the child began to speak it was an eerie mixture of lisps and guttural sounds. The barren women said that no other child had done this before.

'He talks,' they said, 'he talks like the parrot of the Puranas. He is our Kili!'

Thus was Appu born again as Appu-Kili. The five mothers passed him from lap to lap, and soon began to talk like him in those lisps and gutturals. They talked to him endlessly about charming and inane things.

Kuttappu was a migrant, he had moved into Khasak which was the village of his wife, Kali; such migrations were ridiculed as they followed women's trails. But ridicule did not sit well on a man like Kuttappu whose massive musculature was topped with bloodshot eyes and pendulous, sensual lips. Back home in his own mountain village, generations of ancestors had lived and flourished snaring and trading in tigers. Kuttappu gave up that trade because he loved the great cats and abhorred their skinning as regicide. He walked with a slouch, the gait of the striped king; Khasak called him Kuttappu-Nari, Kuttappu the Tiger.

Appu-Kili was growing, but not all of him. When he was ten his arms and legs gave up growing and stayed on in their grotesque childhood. The torso grew, and so did the head, and across the pendulous lips settled a timeless smile. Kuttappu and the sterile women brawled with those who dared suggest that there was something wrong with the child's growth. 'He'll be all right when he grows up,' they said, 'our little prince, our five-hued parrot!'

Neeli alone sorrowed and hid her sorrow from her sisters.

A few days after his visit to Neeli, the Khazi was seated in Aliyar's teashop recounting his duel with a djinn outside Palghat town.

'You all know the tile factory built by the evangelists beside the river, the factory which turns people into Christians, don't you? Well, then you know where the Muslim keeps the sherbet shop? There, behind the shack, where you go down to the river along the unlit path, yes, there! A djinn, most frightful. Any one of you here would have died of fright. But at the tip of my tongue was a great spell, I cast it, and . . . .'

From a corner rose a voice, 'Khazi, good-for-nothing! Wayside magic man!'

It was Kuttappu the Tiger.

'Magician, vagrant!' the Tiger ranted, 'blow away the djinns to your heart's content, but keep your breath off our child!'

The tiger stormed out of the teashop. The story of the djinn was lost, the Khazi was a little unnerved by the burst of blasphemy, and his listeners were puzzled by the Tiger's tearing rage.

The rage lasted the whole day. At sundown the Tiger drank deep and went to sleep.

The sun was high when Kuttappu awoke the next day. The rage was gone, and in its place dawned cold reason. The Khazi was the Sheikh's anointed. Who should come to Kuttappu's rescue if the Sheikh chose to strike? Kuttappu sought Neeli's advice and comradeship. But Neeli was unusually cold, disinclined to talk. Dejected and dazed, the Tiger went to Kuttadan, the oracle of the lower castes. Kuttadan sat before the idol of his goddess and went into a brief trance. Opening his eyes again he said, 'O Tiger, we cannot . . . .' His goddess strictly forbade any quarrel between Hindu and Muslim gods; these gods were the natives of Khasak.

'We cannot set up the gods against themselves,' Kuttadan said, 'we cannot let them brawl.'

Kuttappu pleaded with Kuttadan, it was a matter of life and death; but nothing would make the oracle change his mind.

Kuttappu came away like a sleepwalker, and soon lost all knowledge of where his steps were taking him, until he was startled wide awake on Chetali's foothills! Who had brought him this way, whose was the unseen hand, the unseen leash? There was not a soul within sight or hearing. The Tiger's head swam, and the most casual object or movement struck him with lurid terror—a flurry of dead leaves, a scrabbling rat, a wheeling flight of butterflies. Kuttappu turned and began a slow descent when suddenly a bird chirped and he broke into a run.

He reached the plains, not his home. For reasons he himself did not know, he set out towards Koomankavu. The long walk became a jog, then mortal flight. But Koomankavu was no refuge, as he still sensed the menace of the mountain. He went into a den where they sold illicit alcohol, and came out restored. He found himself on the road to Palghat town. The road was a thin spine of macadam with ploughed-up sides, yet it had the State's majesty and freedom, and the illicit drink was a merciless intoxicant. In a burst of delusion and power Kuttappu threw a challenge, 'Come on, Pootham of Chetali, haunt my backside if you dare!' To make sure the Sheikh got his challenge right, Kuttappu lifted his mundu and bared his behind.

He caught up with a convoy of bullock carts returning to the bazars of Palghat. A Muslim beside whose cart Kuttappu walked asked him, 'Why are you baring your backside?'

The Tiger fell in step with the bullock, and asked the man if he had a bidi to spare. He walked inhaling the pungent tobacco and scratching the bullock's back, and was in no hurry to reply. The man repeated, 'Why did you do it?'

'May I ask for a ride?'

'Get in.'

Kuttappu made himself comfortable, and told the man, 'A pootham is after me.'

'What has the pootham got against you?'

'He is a Muslim demon.'

'That doesn't make any difference,' the man said. 'The government has laid this road for honest users like you and me, it isn't for haunting. Let us see if this pootham dare touch you on the government's freeway.'

'You can't possibly stop him . . . .'

'This is a wager,' the man said. 'I will quit this trade if the demon breaks the rule of the road!'

'What trade?'

'Plying bullock carts.'

The convoy trundled on slowly. It was late afternoon when they reached Palghat town. Kuttappu took leave of the man and let himself loose in the town. On the maidan of the old Sultan's fort a meeting was in progress. The Red Flag fluttered over the speakers who were debating things that concerned the Tiger as well—work and wages. He sat down on the grass among the listeners, but soon lost interest, because his was the more fearsome struggle. He rose and walked away in search of the turgid drink; a couple of draughts more, and Kuttappu was hungry for a fight. The pendulum now moved towards heroism. Kuttappu vowed to return and desecrate the Sheikh's battlements that very night. He hitched a lift in an ancient lorry, which dropped him near Koomankavu. Kuttappu started his walk back to Khasak. He composed an instant song on the road, *'Come pootham, get me if you can, Ta Ra Na Na!'*

It was midnight. The moon dimly lit the pathways; there was no mistaking the evil silhouette far away, the peak of Chetali! Suddenly its contours began to change. To Kuttappu it looked like an old Muslim dervish in a gigantic balaklava. The power of the illicit elixir wore away. Now the clip-clop of the chasing cavalry was loud and clear! The Tiger sweated. The djinns of the Sheikh were right behind him. The Tiger tried to cry for help, but his voice sank. The djinns were coming! Where was Khasak? Home? Kuttappu-Nari hurtled through the moonlight in blind and calamitous flight.

The Twilight

KUTTAPPU LAY TOSSING in delirium. Helplessly, Kali and Neeli went to the Khazi. The Khazi sat in padmasana, the lotus posture. He looked up with soft brown eyes at the women. After a long while he spoke, 'You may now depart!'

Was it pardon or dismissal? The sisters were bewildered. Neeli wanted to talk, to ask. But the stagnant gloom of the mosque intimidated her.

'Go!' said the Khazi, 'Justice will be done. Go!'

At noon the Khazi rose from his padmasana. He burned incense over the nameless graves around the mosque, and took the winding footpath to the village.

An agitated villager informed him, 'O Khazi, the Tiger is dead!'

The Khazi headed for Neeli's house . . . . He stood for a moment at her gate. A deep tremor ran through him. He mumbled a mantra and raised his hand. Then abruptly, he turned and headed back to the marshes.

The following month of Chaitra was the time of flowering and renewal. Twenty years had passed since Neeli had brought forth her cretin son. When the Khazi came as usual to bless the hut, Neeli whispered to him in anxiety, 'O Khazi . . . . '

'What . . . what ails you?'

He saw a shaft of sunlight fall on her lips, saw the lips glisten. She said, 'I am unwell.'

The Khazi grew thoughtful, and was silent. The next day he brought her sweet and bitter concoctions . . . . Chaitra turned to harsher seasons. Neeli's sickness was no longer a distant alarm, she cried out in despair, 'O Khazi!'

He brought rare leaves and roots from Chetali and fermented them.

'Will I be well again, O Khazi?' she asked, savouring the dregs of pleasure.

'You will, *Insha-Allah.*'

Midnight. A mild pain started below her navel, then suddenly it tore through her; Neeli let out a savage cry. The lanterns of Khasak lit and moved towards Neeli's hut. Neeli was rolling naked in a pool of blood. She passed away at dawn. They laid her to rest beside the Tiger.

Appu-Kili slipped out of the house. No one missed him. He sneaked into the dense thickets beside the burial ground and hid there during the day. When night fell he came out and slept beside Neeli's grave. It rained intermittently, and when it stopped, water held in the leaves came down in large drops, piercing cold. He listened to the Kalan Kozhis, nocturnal birds whose eerie call was an omen of death. They perched on branches overhead and crooned to him.

Two days later, Ravi and Madhavan Nair found Appu-Kili's sanctuary. He was covered with the mouldering mud of the graveyard.

'You look ill, little one,' Madhavan Nair said.

Ravi laid his hand over Kili's forehead.

'Doesn't feel too good, Madhavan Nair,' he said, and stooping over the dwarf, asked, 'Why did you sleep out here, Kili?'

Appu-Kili smiled but said nothing.

'Rise, my winged friend,' Madhavan Nair said, 'let us go.'

Appu-Kili began the walk back holding on to Madhavan Nair's and Ravi's forefingers. As soon as they reached the seedling house Ravi wrapped Kili in a blanket, put him to bed in the corridor, and made a cup of steaming coffee. Ravi began rummaging in his medicine chest.

'What are you looking for, Maash?'

'Some medicine for the fever. Can't find any.'

'You can give him tablets if you wish, Maash. But I would recommend no medicine.'

Ravi held the thermometer to the light. The mercury stood at a hundred and four.

Kili!' Ravi called him.

Kili did not open his eyes. He smiled wearily.

Madhavan Nair raised Kili up and Ravi held the coffee to his lips. Kili drank and was asleep again.

'No medicines, Madhavan Nair? What then?'

'Call Kuttadan. These oracles blow away the spirits.'

'But where are the spirits?'

'Right here. Inside the Parrot himself.'

The tailor's attitude worried Ravi. 'This is serious, Madhavan Nair, a temperature of a hundred and four.'

Madhavan Nair sat beside the sleeping dwarf.

'I think there is a doctor in Kozhanasseri,' Ravi said. 'Let me go there and get some medicine.'

'I wouldn't do it, Maash.'

'It's a big responsibility. Let us at least tell his people.'

'His people? The Parrot has no people any more.'

After school Ravi borrowed Aliyar's bicycle and

pedalled to Kozhanasseri over perilous tracks . . . . It was night when Ravi came home with the medicines. A bizarre tableau awaited him. The school yard had been prepared for a ritual, and was lit by large oil-lamps. Appu-Kili sat cross-legged on the ground, and beside him, Madhavan Nair beat a steady tattoo on an ancient drum. In the midst of all this stood Kuttadan clad in a red sari, the raiment of his goddess. The tattoo rose, and as it reached its crescendo Kuttadan smote his head with the curved sword of the oracle. The Devi had possessed him, she spoke in his voice, 'Do not grieve, Neeli-Achchi! And do not tarry here any more!'

Ravi leaned the bicycle on the wall, came over and sat down near Madhavan Nair. Blood clotted on Kuttadan's sword; the voice went on, 'Do not cry, Neeli-Achchi! This cretin is our child. We will not let him be hungry. Go in peace.' And the final astral command, 'Go, go!'

Appu-Kili had fallen flat on his back. Kuttadan laid down the sword and danced, there was gaiety in his mystic steps. Then he stopped dancing, picked up his sword and went home. The villagers too dispersed. Ravi and Madhavan Nair carried Appu-Kili back to the corridor. Rave felt the boy's forehead, the fever had gone. He put away the medicines on the window-sill.

'Did you tell the tree-fellers and their women?' Ravi asked Madhavan Nair.

'I did.'

'No one came for the exorcism?'

'No one, no one.'

The tailor's mind wandered over many things, and he said, 'Poor Neeli had sorrowed much over this cretin. The bond is hard to undo, Maash. She will come again.'

Outside, somewhere in the thickets of the night, Neeli paused in her journey. She turned, she looked back.

Appu-Kili's limbs twitched, and he spoke in his sleep.

With the passing of Kuttappu and Neeli, things began to fall apart. Kali eloped with Pachi's husband. Ramacchar the cattle-broker reported seeing the fugitive couple in a village on the Tamil border. Pachi did not want to stay on in Khasak in shame and loneliness. She moved to the dam site ten miles away, looking for work in the quarries. Days after, Nachi decided to follow her younger sister. That was the last Khasak heard of them. It was rumoured that both were killed in a rock blasting. Another version, spicier, said that both the sisters had been lured by a wily southerner and the trio had fled south. Kochi was taken ill with a uterine disorder, she died bleeding in the big hospital in Palghat town. The large family that once filled the hut was suddenly reduced to two tree-fellers, who, their wives gone, became strangers to each other. They brawled and rioted; the disowned Parrot would look on for a while, and then walk away. Soon, like the last of the elements breaking away from a lifeless body, the two woodsmen went back to their faraway native villages. Appu-Kili wandered about in Khasak. The villagers were pleased to feed him. He went round the little shops that bounded the village square and picked the things he needed, a chunk of palm jaggery from the grocer, a murukku from Aliyar's teashop. Only Maimoona would shoo him away when he asked for bidis. 'Pig!' she would say, 'Go look for stubs!'

That was repudiation, it would make him cry . . . . Orbiting purposelessly, Appu-Kili would come again and again to the abandoned hut. If it pleased him he would enter, and stay for a while. One night the rotted thatch caved in, and the mud walls gave way. The next morning

Appu-Kili came to Madhavan Nair's shop and sat amid the litter of cut pieces.

'You lost your home, little one?' Madhavan Nair consoled the Parrot, 'stay with me.' Kili had not come as a guest or supplicant but he stayed anyway. Kili salvaged an old bed cover and promptly asked Madhav-etta to tie him a cradle. Madhavan Nair knotted the ends of the cloth and hung it from a tamarind branch. It was a cradle big enough for an ox; the child-man lay in it, feet sticking out, and rocked himself to sleep.

Madhavan Nair sat at his sewing machine and looked on the absurd miracle. He remembered his own childhood, long before his uncle Sivaraman Nair had disowned him—he recalled how he and his cousin Kalyanikkutty played 'father-and-mother' under the tamarind trees with pebbles for children and bits of torn cloth for cradles. Dream-children, far, far away. One night the old bed cover gave way. When he woke up, Madhavan Nair saw Appu-Kili squatting beside the heap of cloth that had been his swinging home till some time ago.

'O Avian!' the tailor said, 'how did this come about?'

Aliyar, cleaning his shop for the morning, called out across the square, 'The Parrot had eaten too many vadas last evening—the cradle couldn't take it.'

'O Muslim! Do not say such vile things. There must have been an earthquake last night. Nothing short of it could have torn this cloth.'

'Of course,' laughed Aliyar, 'that is more likely. Khasak hasn't had an earthquake for a long, long time.'

That bed cover was the last length of cloth he had. Madhavan Nair sat worrying.

'Parrot,' he said, 'would you settle for a perching place?'

Appu-Kili smiled and nodded.

That evening Madhavan Nair came to the school with

Appu-Kili. He called out from the gate, 'Maash! Would you give us a perching place?'

'What happened, Madhavan Nair?'

'The earthquake . . . .'

'The earthquake?'

'Yes. It ripped the cradle.'

Madhavan Nair's shop had just the space a man needed, it couldn't accomodate another, so could the winged one perch in the school?

'Alone at night,' Ravi said, 'should he decide to peck me . . . .'

'Have no fear, Maash!'

Madhavan Nair left Kili with Ravi and went back to his shop. He called again the next evening to see how the perch was working.

'I have a wonderful companion now,' Ravi said, 'one who is utterly devoted to letters. Look . . . .'

On the blackboard, over the walls, across the verandah, wherever there was space for graffiti, there appeared the enchanted repetition of the Malayalam consonant, 'Tṭha', written as a rounded 'O'. Madhavan Nair stared in amazement.

'My Parrot!' Madhavan Nair called out.

Appu-Kili came bounding from behind the seedling house, hands full of chalk and coal.

'O noble bird,' Madhavan Nair said, 'you have done our nation proud . . . . Now listen, Maash. Who says my Kili isn't intelligent? I taught him this one letter almost ten years ago . . . .'

'Incredible!'

Appu-Kili went back to his murals, Madhavan Nair made himself comfortable in the easy chair while Ravi sat on the steps leaning on propped up pillows. Madhavan Nair said, 'Sometimes I think we need to learn just one letter . . . .'

'True.'

'I don't say that in jest, Maash.'

Madhavan Nair was remembering his Guru. In the village of Mannoor an unlettered knife-smith went blind. He sat listening to the grind of the honing stone as his apprentice fashioned the knives. The blind one listened to the great dark; people came to him, scores of them, with their afflictions. He discoursed on texts he had never seen, and told his devotees to go back to their homes and see beyond the delusion of seeing . . . . Madhavan Nair concluded his reminiscences but the tailor and the teacher did not move, they sat entranced. The dusk silted on the palms of Khasak.

'Look!' Ravi said.

Appu-Kili stood at the school gate watching tides of homing parrots.

'This little one,' Madhavan Nair said, 'for him it is always the sunset. And he has no nest to reach.'

'Who reaches?'

'True, Maash. No one really does.'

The cretin stood in the twilight of births and deaths. He stood alone. The last flight of parrots receded over the horizon.

The Inspection

A YEAR WENT by. The school opened after the summer break, its strength a fluid twenty. Ravi had spent the holidays in Khasak, trekking up the hills with Madhavan Nair, or sitting up late telling Appu-Kili stories.

Now, he was readying the school for the annual inspection, which was taking place earlier than usual. The Inspector was new. 'What's he like?' Madhavan Nair wondered. 'Strict or lenient?'

'For all I know,' Ravi said, 'he might say, close it down, there aren't enough children!'

'They inflate the rolls—the teaching shops. Can't we put down a dozen dummies on the rolls?'

'The Inspector comes precisely to make sure the rolls aren't faked. And I can't bribe him like the teaching shops do.'

The Inspector of Schools was coming—the word went round. In the outlying slums of untouchables they mistook it for the dreaded vaccinator's visit. The pariah children hid behind hayricks. But in Khasak itself the mood was festive, the front yards of the shacks and the houses around the square were swept clean, and women put on their finery.

Into this carnival walked a frail old man. The black and

silver stubble on his shrivelled cheeks was days old, the customary coat was frayed and clumsily mended. Shod in sandals of crude buffalo hide, he took each step timidly, almost apologetically. This was a poor materialization of the State. Khasak felt let down.

It was the Inspector's peon who salvaged the spectacle for Khasak. He wore a red canvas sash with tassels at the ends, and an outsized brass medallion pinned to it which carried the State's emblem and the legend: *Peon*. Peon, servitor, unarmed food-soldier.

'That man with the red decoration,' Aliyar observed, 'surely he has more powers than the Ispaekkettar.'

'Who can doubt it?' Muthu Pandaram, the saffron-clad mendicant, said. 'Look at the shine of brass!'

'This is no Ispaekkettar,' Kuppu-Achchan commented from the load-rest, 'not a real one.'

'Then what is the reality?' someone from inside the teashop asked.

'It is like the salamander. The hedge lizard, when it's old, and urchins haven't got it, turns into a salamander. So does a maeshter—when he grows very old, he turns into this kind of an Ispaekkettar.'

'Of course,' Alla-Pitcha spoke from the corner he had withdrawn into, 'such is the truth of the salamander.'

Suddenly the tea-drinkers were aware of the mullah's presence. Mutthu Pandaram asked, 'Mollakka, aren't you calling on the Ispaekkettar?'

'No!' the mullah said.

True, he was a part of the school's paraphernalia, and drew a monthly wage. But the battle of the schools, its indelible memories came back to the mullah and 'No!' repeated the priest of Khasak.

The Inspector sat down and dusted the soles of his feet, rubbing them against each other as peasants do.

'A bad headache,' he said, looking up at Ravi.

'Would you like some aspirin, Sir?'

'No, thanks! It was this long trek, and the sun . . . .' The Inspector turned in his chair and pushed the window behind him wide open. 'Fine breeze,' he said. 'And, oh, look what you've got out there . . . .'

'Lotuses,' Ravi said.

The Inspector smiled. Ravi had worked for days to update the registers and documents, and these he set down before the Inspector.

'I shall sign them all anyway,' the Inspector said. 'Let the children go home.'

Ravi dismissed the class and told the children the day after was a holiday too, as it always was after an inspection. For a while the children lingered on in the yard, then spilled away and were gone.

'Sit down, Maash!'

They sat together talking of generalities, of schools and teaching shops.

'Where are you from, Maash?'

Ravi didn't answer. Where am I from, and where am I now, he asked himself, whose face do I see, and whose is this black and silver stubble?

'Prop up the pillows, son,' Ravi heard the dear voice.

'Lean on me, Papa.'

Tardy joints, unwilling tendons.

'Are you comfortable, Papa?'

'Yes, son.'

Ravi could feel the pain his father was concealing. The stubble had grown over two days.

'Shall I give you a shave, Papa?'

'The nurse will do it.'

'Which part of Kerala?' the voice of the old Inspector again.

'Oh, well,' Ravi said, 'our family is from Pattambi, that's not very far away.'

Ravi went into the corridor and came back with a trayful of oranges.

'To beat the heat, Sir.'

After an orange, the Inspector resumed, 'Have you been to the training school?'

'Haven't considered it . . . .'

'Trained teachers are paid reasonably well these days.'

'I suppose so.'

The Inspector leafed through the registers desultorily. 'Maybe you're planning to go to college,' he said. 'It's getting quite expensive though . . . .'

'In a sense I've finished college . . . .'

'Done your college? Then what are you doing here, with this job for matriculates?'

'I didn't take my exams. I was doing an honours course.'

'Where did you go to college? Palghat?'

'Tambaram.'

'The Christian college?'

The college Ravi had attended had an unusually beautiful campus, stretches of shrub and jungle in which hare and porcupine thrived. The teaching and the residential blocks were jewel-red islands amidst this overpowering green. There were clearings covered with grass, like carpets of priceless cashmere.

'What honours were you doing?'

'Astrophysics.'

The lights of the lab came back to Ravi, the lenses that sought to look out far, very far, and space which looked in through every aperture, to strike the dark of the abyss.

'Parents alive?'

'Lost my mother very early. My father used to be a doctor in a plantation. For some years he has been ill. I've a stepmother, and two stepsisters studying abroad . . . .'

Suma and Rama, the stepsisters, looked out of the family album with the eyes of strangers. Where had he left that album, where in the hollows of the unquiet mind had he abandoned his sisters?

'I had a daughter, Maash . . .' the Inspector said.

Two wanderers, they were meeting in this caravansarai and exchanging sad biographies. The old man told Ravi about his daughter, the talented first-born for whose sake he had stopped his other children from going beyond school—he could afford to see only one child through university. In the weeks before the final examinations, Dhatri wouldn't put the books away. She would read far into the night, sometimes into the next dawn. With just a week to go, fatigued beyond endurance, Dhatri nodded asleep at the sight of print. She would shake herself awake, and smile to cheer her father who stayed awake with her through those gruelling nights. One night Dhatri went out into the yard to where the well water was kept in large earthen urns. The father heard the sound of water being poured, he peered out. 'Dousing your head?' he was aghast. The girl said, 'Can't get the sleep off the lids, father.'

He thought of her heavy tresses and how they would be difficult to dry in the night.

'Shall I mop your hair for you, my little one?'

'Oh, no, father. You go in and sleep for a while.'

'Take care to dry you hair well.'

He had heard her laugh in reply, a tired, indulgent laugh. When he came back to their little study, he had found Dhatri slumped over the table, fast asleep. The next evening she complained of a pain in the chest. The pain grew, the inflammation galloped through the lungs. Dhatri had died.

'You said your father is ailing, didn't you, Maash?'

'Yes, Sir. It's a rheumatoid condition. Half the body is paralysed.'

'Pain and dependence . . . .'

'The way everyone goes.'

The Inspector smiled again, turned towards the registers to attest all the absurd and voluminous information they held.

'Does your father stay in Pattambi?'

'No, Sir. We have a house in Ooty, in the hills, built during my father's plantation days . . . .'

The land around the house was a generous expanse, a whole hillside. A neat drive took you to the porch. Inside the house was sculptured woodwork, carpeted flooring, hand-cut crystal, and a grand piano that had been silent for years. It was in this house that he had sinned with his stepmother. He was at college then; he had come home for the holidays. That was ten years ago.

'Maash,' the Inspector said, 'I can't imagine a bright young man like you not taking the exams. An honours degree all packed and waiting to be picked up! I'd like to see you in those robes, holding the scroll.'

Ravi remembered the visiting professor, the Princetonian, who had called him over to the college guest-house one day.

'That paper of yours,' the visitor had said, 'your professor passed it on to me . . . .' The bass voice and the grin spreading across the wide jaws had been friendly.

'Engrossing,' the visitor went on, 'although I suspect your basic physics is all wrong.'

'I've never been strong on my facts, Sir.'

'But do you realize you aren't pitting Hindu wisdom against Western science. You're doing something more audacious. You are using your own wisdom.'

They had talked and ranged over dim riddles, and it was as if the Ganga had risen before them as the deluge, as time; in her mystic reaches the Truth lay hidden.

An evening in their favourite clearing on campus. Padma had told Ravi, 'The Princeton person came home, and he and papa talked most of the time about you. He feels you are a one-man revolt against all post-Galilean science.'

Padma's father had been Ravi's professor. Ravi's despair had begun anew: I am destined not to know and yet this curse is on me—the knowledge that Truth is, and that it is forbidden to man. In pain and sorrow he had turned to his childhood and the noontide wrapped him in its fiery gold. There was no seeking, the skies were lucid and loving again, love came in visions of Kalpaka husks and diademed serpents.

'What does the American want to do to me, Padma?'

'Feed you, fatten you, I suppose.'

'Padma, if I do not get through this examination?'

She had been annoyed.

'Here I give you good news, and you tease me wickedly in return.'

'Padma . . . ' he had begun helplessly. He spoke within himself, what am I trying to accomplish scanning galactic distances and reading the bands of colour split out of stellar lights by lowly prisms? Doesn't my sin lie within?

The exams, their feverish nearness. The hostels had stayed awake. Ravi lay down, giving himself up to the caverns of the sky.

Days later.

'My moody lover,' Padma had said, 'let me take you out

tomorrow. The sea breeze will do you good.'

'The Marina?'

'Further up, near Luz. Out there it isn't too crowded. The old people are dining out.'

On the sands, the next day—

Ravi had pulled out a letter and given it to Padma. *I'm not too ill, my son,* it had read, *though things go spinning at times. Days go on, one day like any other. Your Chittamma wheels me into the verandah to watch the sunset. More than my illness, another, greater sadness is on me when I see the sun go. What am I sad about? All twilight is sadness . . . .*

The dusk had grown darker, colder. A flight of night birds high above had caught the city's glow and shone like dim meteors . . . .

It was afternoon when Ravi and the Inspector reached Koomankavu. The last bus to Palghat town was waiting. They treated themselves to glasses of sherbet mixed by the talkative vendor.

'You in this lost village,' the Inspector said, 'strange are the ways of destiny, Ravi.'

Strange indeed; untrodden paths called to Ravi with mesmeric power. The night before the examination, he had slipped out of the hostel. The journey had begun.

The journey into the vast unquiet universe, watched by faces in railway compartments, tolerant and incurious. In the nights Ravi had curled up on luggage racks and slept to the soft beat of the rails. The names of railway stations had changed, their scripts had changed. Then on the road, up the high ranges, past hairpin bends in gasoline-perfumed buses. The roadway dust had changed colour, sunrise and sunset had changed places, directions had been lost in an assailing infinity. The journey took him through cheerless suburbs, through streets of sordid trades, past cacti villages and lost townships of lepers, and Ashramas where, in saffron beds, voluptuous swaminis lay in wait for nirvana. And at last, this respite, this Sarai in Khasak . . . .

'We should see each other again,' the Inspector said.

Ravi held the old man's hands, the gnarled, suffering palms.

'Certainly, Sir.'

'I retire in the middle of this year.'

'You'll still be in Palghat. It's no great distance.'

'One never knows, Maash. The ones who stay near are at times the farthest to reach. Who knows, this might well be our last meeting!'

They laughed. The Inspector and the peon boarded the waiting bus.

'How is the headache?'

'The winds have cured it.'

'Namaskaram!'

The bus moved. Ravi waited for the dust to settle. He bought a bundle of palm fibre torches, and began the long trek back to Khasak. Soon it was dark. Ravi lit a torch and waved it in the wind. It broke into a brilliant flame.

The brook was still warm when Ravi got back. He

undressed and sat immersed in the brisk current for a while, then rose and took the footpath to the seedling house . . . . As he went to bed, the cry came through the silent night.

Allaho Akbar!
Allaho Akbar!

That was the muezzin's call for the last prayer. God, Ravi said, in a voiceless chant. No longer was the word harsh or distant. He rose for a draught of water, came back to bed and was quiet. The muezzin's call had punctuated his turbulence.

Outside, the night lay inebriated with its vastness. The wind was on the palms of Khasak. Beyond the reaches of the village late wayfarers waved their fibre torches, pulses of flame and ember. Like stricken space ships signalling distress with their incandescent antennae, they continued their desolate journey.

Dragonflies

SIVARAMAN NAIR HADN'T come to greet the Inspector, his interest in the school had waned. Every little thing soured him. He walked about carrying brittle angers whose causes he could not determine. He needed someone to blame it all on. He chose the Muslim. But he found no listeners—neither Hindu nor Muslim was prone to quarrel, as both their religions teemed with the same tender absurdities. The history of Khasak was the great oral legend; that, and a shared indigence held Khasak together. With the coming of the school, Sivaraman Nair had cheered up, here at last was a symbol, a centre, for his angry fantasies. The mullah was against the school, yet the school survived. Ravi was unaware of this private battle. The young teacher had even struck a deal with the mullah, allowing time for the Muslim children to come to school after they had done their Koranic lessons at the madrassa. Sivaraman Nair's disenchantment grew when he found Ravi fraternising with Madhavan Nair, the wayward nephew who had disgraced the family by becoming a tailor, an artisan. Sivaraman Nair's visits to the school grew less frequent.

Ravi was pleasantly surprised, therefore, when the landlord appeared at the bamboo gate, opening and closing it with great deliberation. One look, and Ravi sensed trouble. The old face was wracked with incoherent grievance. Sivaraman Nair declined the chair Ravi drew for him and sat down on the steps instead, partly in protest and partly for the warmth of the sunset on the stucco. Ravi came over and sat down beside him.

'You don't look too well, Sivaraman Nair,' Ravi said.

'How can I be?' came the mystifying retort.

Sivaraman Nair began to pant and sweat, the blood rushing inside him. A middle-aged Muslim woman was at the well, drawing water for Ravi's improvised bath and kitchen.

'Who is she, Maash?'

'Chand Umma, my servant.'

Sivaraman Nair paused to make a notch in his memory, and after a few bitter and speechless moments, turned on Ravi, 'So it is a Bouddha woman again . . . .'

'Yes. And it is no fault of mine—not that I have anything against Muslims. I told you I wanted a servant, you couldn't find me one.'

Sivaraman Nair realized the fault was his, and embarrassedly diverted the conversation. 'Sometimes I wonder if your District Board is bankrupt. Can't they employ a caretaker on a sensible wage?'

'The Board is stupid, they make a niggardly grant and expect me to hire the school's all-purpose handyman . . . .'

'And where is that money?'

'You know where, Sivaraman Nair. The mullah is our handyman—on paper.'

'And you pay him the grant money, and spend out of your pocket to hire this servant—'

The logic was becoming more and more muddled.

The conversation flagged again until Ravi asked impatiently, 'Sivaraman Nair, what are we talking about?'

'About infidels, about Yavanas, Bouddhas, your new-found kin.'

Ravi laughed in relief.

'Don't laugh, Maash. Hand me that money, I shall buy oil and anoint the snake gods who could take away your sins.'

The woman had finished for the day. Sivaraman Nair watched her go, gazing at her manically. Soon he too rose to leave. He walked across the yard, stumbling beneath the burden of his own body. His anger, his confusion wasn't about the school or domestic help any longer, but was the residue of unknown and insane wars.

It was Madhavan Nair who had sent her to the seedling house. Chand Umma stood before Ravi, a pale and sad woman with dark patches on her cheeks and around her eyes, marks of the underfed.

'Umma, can you help me with the cooking?' Ravi asked.

'I can, Saar.'

'You may eat here if you like.'

She had not expected that—she was overwhelmed, and stood caressing the unkempt hair of her little son who hid behind her.

'My first born, Saar,' she said bashfully.

'Your name, young man,' Ravi said.

'Tell the Saar,' his mother coaxed. The boy peeped out and answered, 'Kunhu Nooru.'

'Good boy,' Ravi said, 'how is it that I don't see you in the school? How old are you?'

'Eight,' the mother answered.

Ravi noticed the boy had no shirt, and all he wore was a strip of threadbare cloth round his waist. Ravi took out some money and gave it to Chand Umma.

'This is for a shirt and shorts,' he said. 'Give it to Madhavan Nair and tell him I want it done soon. And I'm putting Nooru on the rolls right away.'

The teacher and the mother and son fell silent for a while. Then Chand Umma spoke, her voice tremulous, 'We are under a curse, Saar.'

'Curse?' Ravi laughed. 'I'll take care the curse does not follow Nooru to school.'

'*Yaa Allah*!' she said.

The next evening Kunhu Nooru presented himself in his new shirt and shorts. Trailing behind him was his four-year-old sister Chandu Mutthu, with no clothes on.

'Sorry, little one,' Ravi said, 'I left you out. I'll tell Madhavan Nair to make some frocks for you.'

'Don't want,' Chandu Mutthu lisped.

'Don't want the frocks?'

'Give it to the boy.'

'Don't you like frocks with printed flowers?'

'Let the boy grow up fast.'

Chand Umma stood watching, listening. She broke into a shrill laugh, then wiped away her tears. She said, 'It is her nature.'

At home, where they made do with thin rice gruel most of the time, Chand Mutthu would dip her hand into her earthen bowl, gather up the little sediment of rice grains and put it into Kunhu Nooru's bowl.

'Umma,' she would tell her mother, 'let the boy grow up fast.'

'*Insha Allah*, my little one,' Chand Umma would say, 'and then all your sorrows will end.'

'When will the boy grow big, Umma?'

'By the next Eid, my child.'

'When is the next Eid, Umma?'

'After four moons, my precious.'

And so they waited, mother and daughter, for the boy to grow up . . . .

Soon Kunhu Nooru had his slate and pencil. He sat by the little oil wick doing his homework. Chand Umma stood in the weak shadows of the lamp and watched her first-born write on the framed slate, rub and write again, letters, numerals, none of which she understood. She stood a long while, lost in the wondrous happenings in their home. Kunhu Nooru felt her adoration on his skin and hair, and was uneasy.

'What's it, Umma?'

'Nothing, my precious.'

Ravi was reclining in his easy chair after school. Chandu Mutthu had curled up on the steps and was watching her mother's dreary walk to the well and back.

'Umma . . . .'

'Yes, my child?'

'Tired, Umma?'

'No, my little one.'

Chandu Mutthu repeated the questions each time her mother walked back with the filled pitcher.

'Umma . . . .'

'Yes, my sweet?'

'When the boy grows up, you won't have to carry water, Umma?'

'*Insha Allah,* my precious.'

'When will it be, Umma?'

'When we see the next Eid moon . . . .'

Ravi lay in his easy chair, listening. By now he was familiar with this engrossing dialogue of hope and the magic calendar of the moons.

Once on a weekend he bought chocolate at the small

township of Kozhanasseri. He gave four pieces each to brother and sister. Ravi teased, 'Chandu Mutthu, don't you want to give away your share to the boy?'

Chandu Mutthu hesitated, then after deep thought held out one piece for Kunhu Nooru.

'Little one,' Kunhu Nooru said, 'you keep your share.'

Relieved, she withdrew the chocolate. Ravi laughed. Chand Umma came in to sweep, in time to witness the temptation of the little one. A tender sadness filmed her eyes. She said, 'Don't get them used to chocolate, Saar. When you move out of here, my children will fret and pine.'

Days went by, the patches on Chand Umma's cheeks began clearing, and soon disappeared altogether, the skin cleansed deep.

Sivaraman Nair came again, a month after the last angry visitation.

'I thought you had forgotten your way here,' Ravi said, making a bid at small talk, but Sivaraman Nair was in no mood for pleasantries.

He asked bluntly, 'So she is still here?'

'Who?'

'The Bouddha woman.'

'Yes,' Ravi was defiant.

'Maash,' the landlord began ominously, 'I have come to tell you something, though it is none of my concern. Why are you living with this Muslim woman?'

Ravi was aghast. 'Who's spreading this damned lie?'

'Aren't you living with her?'

'But who told you this lie?'

'Let it be anybody. Haven't you put her up in this seedling house of a school? Why don't you own up?'

'Own up what?'

'Whatever,' Sivaraman Nair slunk back into the refuge of senility. He rose to go, but paused to mop the profuse sweat that showed on his close-cropped hair and the nape of his neck.

'O Mahamaya!' he muttered, 'what foul sins am I destined to witness!'

For a moment Ravi contemplated calling Sivaraman Nair back—he could reason it out with the enfeebled patriarch. Then, realizing the futility of the exercise, he sat down to watch him go.

The day after was a holiday. Chand Umma came a little before midday to cook. Ravi followed her into the corridor which was his kitchen as well as bedroom. Ravi sat down on the cot. Chand Umma stooped over the stove. She was tense and did not look at him.

'Umma!' Ravi sought her attention. For some reason she had anticipated the encounter and came and stood before Ravi without demur.

'Sit down.'

She chose to sit on the floor.

'What's this lie I hear about us?' Ravi asked. 'Who has told Sivaraman Nair that you are my mistress?'

'Kuppu-Acchan,' she said in a low, parched whisper.

'What has Kuppu-Acchan got against me?'

'It is his nature.'

The stove had gone out.

'Let me go light the stove,' she said.

'Sit down!'

The sun came in through the solitary glass tile on the roof. The light fell in an epiphanic beam on her face where the patches had given way to pure translucence.

'How long ago was it that you lost your husband?'

'Four years. Soon after I had delivered Chandu Mutthu.'

As she said this a great sadness was on her face, the veil of the obscure curse . . . .

It had happened in the lost time of Khasak, but it lived on, a brooding, avenging sorrow. The great tamarind tree which stood on the edge of the burial marsh was witness to that sorrow. Old beyond measure, Khasak believed the tree wouldn't die until it was redeemed in some way. It was beneath this tree, in that lost time, that an old, widowed astrologer and his daughter had built their hut. A company of white cavalry came there in search of water for their camels. They killed the old star-watcher and raped the daughter. They left her to die on the marsh and went their way towards the mountains, but as they went up the foothills scorpions crawled into their battle fatigues and black cobras bit the camels. Camels and riders perished in the wild, and the loam of the mountain settled over their bones. The dead girl rose from the marsh and made the tamarind tree her abode. Worshipped as a Devi, she was the guardian of the chaste. The tamarind tree grew to enormity and, despite its great age, bore fruit in abundance. There were wandering tamarind merchants and their climbers and sellers, who came from Koomankavu and elsewhere, and the harvest overhead was rich, yet few dared to climb up. For the trunk was covered with slippery lichen and the canopy infested with venomous ants. But if the climber had a chaste wife the Devi would turn the lichen into firm footholds, and the ants would make way. The men did not want to be brought to the test, so each season the sweet and sour fruit fell into the marsh or was eaten by flights of bats . . . . Four years ago, Chand Umma's husband had stood at the foot of the tree and looked up. He was dazzled, there was a fortune to be plucked. He began to climb. The villagers found him the next day sprawled over the edge of the marsh, blood still oozing from the splintered skull and hordes of ants, glimmering violet and magenta, marauding over the eyes and genitals. It was on that day that Chand Umma's father left Khasak to become a wandering fakir.

This punitive widowhood brought on exclusion, and unbearable loneliness. It was custom for the villagers to help each other mend the thatch of their roofs, but now none came to mend hers. The rotting palmyra fronds of the thatch flapped in the monsoon winds, and lightning filled the hut with cold blue fire. In this hut the mother and daughter prayed for the boy to grow up . . . .

Ravi made Chand Umma tell the story all over again. The epiphanic sunbeam vanished. When the recital was over, Ravi asked, 'Umma, do you believe the Devi was punishing?'

She met his gaze with stern and accusing eyes. Then courage gave way to shame, and Chand Umma was seized with a spasm of crying. Ravi lifted her chin up, he found himself wiping her tears from around her eyes and her cheeks. He held her by the shoulders and tried to seat her on the cot. Chand Umma disengaged herself and stood leaning against the wall, her chest heaving. Ravi could not reckon how long that tableau lasted. She came over and sat beside him.

Ravi laid a gentle hand over her shoulder.

'You do not know, Saar—' she began.

'Do not know what?'

'The sorrow of little children.'

Ravi's hand slid down from her shoulder. It was a calm noon outside, and from within its wondrous hollow came the noises of children at play, the strange warbling of a migrant bird, the tired creaking of an ungreased cart-wheel. She snuggled closer, cheerlessly.

'Umma!'

That was Kunhu Nooru, standing at the entrance to the corridor. Chand Umma got up from the cot. She looked at the dead stove.

'I go now, Saar . . . .'

She did not cook that day.

Ravi walked down to Aliyar's teashop. The aappams smelt of the toddy the dough was leavened with. Kuppu-Acchan was basking on the load-rest.

'Let us have some tea together,' Ravi invited.

'Aayee, aayee!' the carrier of tales said, 'Not for me.'

'Oh, come on!'

'Well, if you insist—Aliyar take out a couple of aappams as well.'

'Here, hungry ghost,' the teashop keeper put the aappams and tea on the load-rest. Kuppu-Acchan fell upon the food and drink greedily, his face contorted. He called out to Ravi inside the teashop, 'Kutti, the sun is mild, and the brooks are full. Shall we go fishing?'

'Not me, Kuppu-Acchan,' Ravi answered.

'This is the time when the big fish come up for the sun.'

'Leave me out, Kuppu-Acchan.'

Ravi stepped out of the teashop. He paused to take a closer look at Khasak's frail slanderer.

'Merry fishing, Kuppu-Acchan!'

Ravi walked away towards the paddies. Appu-Kili was hunting amid the screw pines for dragonflies.

'Wan daagonfies, Etto?' Kili asked with his abysmal lisp.

'Not now, my Parrot,' Ravi said, patting the cretin's enormous head. 'Bring me one when you come home to sleep.'

As he walked Ravi went over the events of that day again, the desire, the apathy and fulfilment, the invasive curiosity. Where was he, and what was he in this bewildering swirl of live and dead happenings?

Ravi walked over the ridge; overhead, a million dragonflies sallied forth into the bland sun. Memories of the dead, the dead pining for miraculous reprieves. Ravi walked beneath the canopy of little wings. Khasak lay dreaming all about him. In that experience he prayed for an end to Chand Umma's curse. The ridge stretched before him becoming infinite, spanning recurrence and incarnation.

The Ruins

NO ONE REMEMBERED the Kuppu-Acchan of the past, youthful Kuppu the toddy-tapper; no dragonfly carried the memories of the living. Kuppu-Acchan himself found recollection burdensome . . . .

A mid-noon fifteen years ago in Kuppu's toddy-shop. Custom was thin and Kuppu full of misgiving. As he sat gazing far out across the yellowing paddies, he caught sight of the postman, Kelu Menon, walking down the ridge towards Khasak.

He walked into the shop and sat down to a mugful of toddy and a length of roasted goat's gut.

'Can't think of a better refreshment,' said Kelu Menon cheerily, 'but how long will you keep this open?'

Kuppu's wife Kallu peeped in from the living quarters at the back. 'We will not close this down,' she said.

Kuppu said nothing.

'This is the new law,' said the postman, speaking now as part of the government. 'We can't let the law be disobeyed.'

Days after this, Kuppu walked beneath the palms at sunset. He touched the palms and divined the sap flow, up the trunks to the buds on top. He tapped the sap and brewed it into sweet-sour toddy. He sold this toddy in his little shop. A trade, an honest and fearless living; try as he might he could not understand why anyone should make it impossible. He sadly watched the magnificent palms turn to silhouettes in the onrushing dusk.

Kuppu kept his shop open. No one came there to drink anymore. Kuppu roamed the palm groves; he could climb and tap twenty palms a day; he wore the tapper's mark of power—callouses the colour of gold on his hands and chest.

The villagers dared not reason with him; the only one he would listen to was Madhavan Nair, younger than him by many years. They respected each other as skilled workers, free people. When Madhavan Nair saw Kuppu that evening amidst the palms, he realized he was witnessing a mime of torment, the palm-climber's passion play.

'I have done much wrong in my life,' Kuppu began.

'Who hasn't?' protested Madhavan Nair.

'I have. But I haven't taken a life. I nearly did it last evening. Can you guess what Mayandi advised me to do?'

The tailor stood still, listening.

'Mayandi wants me to brew fake toddy from waste and poison . . .' said Kuppu in a great rage.

Kuppu stood leaning against a palmyra; Madhavan Nair marvelled at the tapper's musculature and at the honour of the toiling man. The palm winds blew a cool breeze and quietened Kuppu.

They walked in the cool night; the tailor talked and reasoned.

'What should I do?' asked the tapper again.

'Close it,' said Madhavan Nair gently.

And so ended the epic of the toddy-tapper, an epic from

other times, when flying serpents rested on palm tops during their mysterious journeys. The tapper made an offering of sweet toddy to please these visitants. He left flowers at the foot of the palm for the clan's well-being. In those times the tapper did not have to climb, the palm bent down for him. It was when a tapper's woman lost her innocence that the palm ceased to bend . . . .

Kuppu's wife Kallu was from Yakkara, a village a few miles from Khasak. The daughter of a prosperous tenant-farmer, she was the youngest of seven sisters; the farmer had married off six of them, and when Kallu's turn came, there was little left of the family's gold and money.

That was how she came to Khasak as the bride of a tapper, one whose station was lower than that of a tenant-farmer. A bride of fourteen, she had come away from the roomy family farmhouse, the yard around it, the stables where the grey buffalo calves would shake their heads and flare their nostrils in recognition. She found her husband a loner and the house beset with dust and cobwebs, moss and trash. She suppressed a sob, and swore she would move her man to decisive enterprise. Within weeks of the marriage Kallu said, 'Let us take some land on tenure.' Kuppu was mindful of every wish of the child-wife, though he hated the feudal humiliation of tenancy. He went into it for her sake, but gave it up at the very first harvest when the landlord spoke rudely to him. Still Kallu would not give up.

'There is a toddy shop here,' she told him in bed one night, 'that closed down long ago. Let us bid for it.'

Kuppu found her irresistible, but equally compelling was the call of the wind-swept palms that resounded in the night.

'I cannot give them up,' he said. 'They love me.'

Kallu pulled him back to see him better, this man who turned his enormous power into tenderness. Then she drew him close and giggled, 'I am jealous!'

Kallu fancied the palms as big black giantesses tossing their locks in the wind.

'I will tap,' he said.

'We will have both,' she said. 'I can see to the shop when you are on the palms.'

For her the toddy-shop was a mark of class. Of course it was classier to be a farmer, but she had heard of men who got rich vending toddy. In this ceaseless fantasy she became rich, and dressed the way the rich did; ornaments glittering all over her, she went to Yakkara, to her father's farm, to the calves which snorted in fond memory . . . . The shop dragged on for years on inadequate custom, and Kallu never made that jewelled journey.

After the shop was closed down, Kuppu set out for the palm grove one morning, in tapper's attire—the shield of buffalo hide for the chest, the broad knife in its scabbard hung at the back from the girdle. The mullah, on his morning walk through the fields, was alarmed by this armed apparition.

'Where are you going, Kuppu?' he asked hesitantly.

Kuppu was jolted by this query from the world of reality.

'Aw,' he said, 'to cut fronds . . . .'

That was not the season for mending thatches, but the mullah questioned him no further. He turned to watch the tapper walk away, and said a prayer to save this man of honour from relapsing into hallucination. In the grove, Kuppu climbed his favoured palm, the queen among his black mistresses; he sat astride the stem of a frond, contemplating nothingness; the wind spun the mountain mists around him, and the earth seemed far away . . . . In the house below, Kallu dusted the big earthen urns which had once held the brew of their labour and hope, now destroyed by the Temperance Law and the bootlegger. The smell of toddy still lingered in the long-dried earthen urns, perhaps its astral replica; sadness came over her. She went into the backyard and looked over great distances, she fancied she saw the little bridge in Yakkara, the gate of her father's farm, the fruit trees along the hedges, the stable which housed her mute kin. She stepped back into her own house again, into its stark solitude. Her husband would not climb down from the palm until the insane spell was over. Her teenaged son worked in a tea plantation in the hill country. Soon even the spectral scent would dry in the urns. The little jewellery she had brought with her was either pawned or sold. Now it felt like an unburdening. All that was left were her silver anklets. She tucked them into her tiny betel basket. She looked out on the front yard—the old slippery moss had returned. Kallu had come in through the front door. She went out through the back. With memories left behind like the pawned jewels, Kallu left Khasak.

The Palghat countryside was in the throes of temperance. Soon primitive alchemists took over the inebriation trade. Brewing and distilling began with substances picked up at random, from confectioners' essences to insects and vermin. Attendance dropped in the rural schools, and often when a teacher asked why a certain pupil had not turned up, the children would answer, 'He's gone hunting centipedes, Saar!'

The most popular drink was fermented wash blended with ammonium sulphate, which the government generously distributed as manure. It came closest to natural toddy. However, there was one embarrassing hazard with the sulphate brew—an overdose of the chemical brought on an upset stomach instantly.

Kuppu stood alone in this welter of deceit, he cursed the Temperance Law as the mother of anarchy. Kallu was its victim. His long spells of hallucination ended, he withdrew into his hut. He hung the chest armour and the tapper's knife on the wall, and never touched them again, and in good time big hairy spiders found a home behind the uncured hide. In the hut that was once their home and toddy shop, Kuppu lay down for days on end in the gathering dust and litter, for days on end he went without food. Then, he wandered through Khasak, at each appearance looking thinner and more desiccated than at the one before; no one took note, no dragonfly carried the memories of the living. Sometimes if the wind swept him on, he went up to Chetali. He came back, and gave himself up to the contemplation of the image that was to be the only image in his mind for years to come. Kallu's parents were dead, leaving behind a rheumatic grandmother. Kuppu worked himself into an insane despondency in which he could see things the way he wanted to; he saw Kallu bathing in Yakkara's rivulet, seated on the rocks now, sun-drying herself, bare-breasted, with a scanty towel drawn round her waist, like Narayani. The boys from the nearby tile factory loitered beside the rivulet, they ogled and whistled. They whistled in the nights around the house of the rheumatic grandmother. Kallu in the rivulet haunted Kuppu. The image rotted in his mind and then seeped out to envelop him. Kuppu curled up and slept through fifteen years of decay . . . .

No one knew for certain when he appeared on the

load-rest in front of Aliyar's shop. It was as if he had always been there. A lock of sick brown hair falling over his forehead, cheeks drawn into the face's toothless cavern, head tucked in between bent knees, infinitely old, he picked on passers-by or those inside the teashop and began some salacious story.

'You know,' he would start off, 'Pangelan's wife is with child, the ninth month, and poor Pangelan has so much work in the Tamil country that he has been away for almost two years. Of course, none of my concern . . . .'

Kuppu-Acchan could almost see the scandal sail downwind, see if flower and multiply. Often Aliyar took out a pot of bitter tea and odd bits of crispies, and clapped his hands. 'Come and peck, old crow,' Aliyar would say, affectionately endowing the village gossip with the mystic powers crows were supposed to possess and for which reason they were made offerings of food in propitiation rites.

A day after Sivaraman Nair accused Ravi of living with his servant, Madhavan Nair walked up to the load-rest with this taunt, 'So you can't resist a juicy lie, can you?'

'Hai, hai, Madhava! Wasn't I talking to the wind?'

'Just stay on the load-rest, and keep your fist closed tight.'

'What else?' Aliyar spoke from behind the samovar. 'If he opens his fist his soul would fly away!'

'Very well,' Madhavan Nair said, 'have some tea. Aliyar, that's on me.'

'Hai, hai! Why don't you get me a murukku to go with the tea?'

'Are you turning into another Appu-Kili?'

Khasak was used to teasing Kuppu-Acchan. An ugly

grin spread through the stubble beneath the beaked nose, for one brief moment, like a cinder fanned by a freak wind. Inside the teashop, Madhavan Nair was touched by memories of the palm grove, of the magnificent toddy-tapper who stood like an angry sentinel over the honour of his calling.

The tailor really had not meant to taunt the old man who now sat on the load-rest to receive the crude mockery of the whole village.

The conversation inside the shop turned to migrant fish. The fish entered the brook, swam upstream, and crawled over the mire to breed in the Araby tank.

'All you have to do,' Aliyar was telling Madhavan Nair, 'is to take a gunny sack and gather them. At night if you show a light, they come to you in shoals.'

'Good,' said the decrepit voice from the load-rest, 'I am ready!'

Aliyar peeped out of his shop to look up at the load-rest. He said, 'Nobody asked you.'

'Hai, hai, Aliyar . . . .'

Kuppu-Acchan did go fishing on rare occasions, all by himself. Tired of the slime of gossip, tired of his grotesque perch, he would get down from the load-rest and walk beside the brook, walk a long way upstream in the sun, and stand in knee-deep water like the sarus crane. The fish would swim by, the curious little ones would nibble at his shins. Kuppu-Acchan would stand still, fish-trap still nestling in the crook of his arm, terrified and elated by what he saw. The fish would slip by like all young and cunning things; yet as he watched the sky reflected in the water, he would be the rider of the sky again, and now what slid past his shins would not be fish but shoals of little clouds.

Kuppu-Acchan overheard Aliyar talking to Madhavan Nair about the migrant fish. He got down from the load-rest and walked about in the mild sun. In the evening he came up to the seedling house and said abruptly, 'Maeshtar, you are eating with me tonight.'

'My food is cooked already.'

'Oh, no! Tonight it will be fish curry in my little home. I can carry away your cooked food so it does not go to waste.'

'Kuppu-Acchan, do you insist?'

Kuppu-Acchan had already gone in and packed the food. There was nothing Ravi could do but go.

Night had fallen when he got there. Ravi sat down on a mat spread out on the narrow verandah. Kuppu-Acchan turned towards the room that opened on to the verandah and called out, 'My little girl, see who has come to supper.'

The woman peeped out, then emerged in informal attire, a short mundu and brassiere.

'Kesi, my daughter-in-law,' Kuppu-Acchan introduced her. She brought water in a bronze kindi for the guest to wash his hands and feet.

'Kutti,' Kuppu-Acchan said, 'would you like a drink—jasmine moonshine?'

Confectioner's flavouring essence; Ravi was hesitant.

'There is nothing to fear,' Kuppu-Acchan said.

'It is a safe drink,' Kesi added her reassurance.

She brought three china bowls. Ravi waited.

'I forgot all about it,' Kuppu-Acchan said, grinning obscenely.

'Forgot what?'

'The drink—I forgot to get the drink.'

'We needn't drink, Kuppu-Acchan. It is all right with me.'

'Oh no!' said Kuppu-Acchan, rising. 'I can't dishonour my guest. Give me ten rupees, Maeshter-kutti.'

Ravi handed him the money, perplexed, and watched

his host hobble away into the dark. When the old man was gone, Kesi came over and sat on Ravi's mat.

'He talks of you so much,' she said. 'He has long wanted to bring you over for a meal.'

Ravi mumbled formal thanks, then got up and leaned on the wall. As the conversation meandered, Ravi asked her, 'When will your husband return?'

'He is in the Tamil country, up in the mountains, plucking tea leaves. No one knows when he will come back. He wasn't staying here anyway. Closer to his mother. The old one was alone here, so he brought me over some time ago.'

Kuppu-Acchan returned with a large bottle of pernicious wash.

'Do you want a sip, girl?' he asked Kesi as she unhooked and hooked her brassiere to be as properly dressed as possible.

'Hai, hai! Isn't Appa making me naughty?' she giggled.

'If the bootlegger has used too much varnish,' Kuppu-Acchan said, 'we are all dead or stricken blind. So take a neat, quick gulp, Kutti!'

They drank generous mouthfuls. Ravi savoured its infamy and said, 'It feels great, Kuppu-Acchan! We can see and we aren't dead.'

Suddenly Kuppu-Acchan stood up again. 'I've forgotten . . . .'

'Forgotten what?' asked Ravi.

'The fish,' Kuppu-Acchan said. He took the bamboo fish-trap off the hook and was gone again . . . . When he reached the teashop it was deserted. Aliyar was inside tallying the day's accounts. The samovar had died down.

'O Muslim,' Kuppu-Acchan asked, 'where is my little Nair?'

'The tailor said he didn't want to fish. I too am in no mood.'

'You were the ones who got me into this . . . .'

'Of course not.'

Kuppu-Acchan collapsed into his familiar knots, and sat on the doorway to nag Aliyar. The final tally was done and Aliyar turned on his tormentor. Then, unable to stand the low drumming monotony of the torment, Aliyar gave in.

The two set out for the Araby tank.

'Old one,' Aliyar said, 'do you know where we are going? To the Araby tank. The place is choking with ghosts.'

'Hai, hai, O kin of Sayed Mian Sheikh, don't scare me this night.'

They were now near the burial ground of the Muslims.

'O shaven-headed Muslim . . .' Kuppu-Acchan nagged.

'What's it? And stop talking about my scalp. It touches my religion and I might decide to kill you.'

'I shall not talk of it, round-head. But the night is getting cold.'

'What else can the night do?'

'Hai, hai! It is drilling into my bones.'

'Who invited you?'

'Wait here, round-head! Let me rush home and get my blanket!'

'This is crazy!'

The mist was descending and Kuppu-Acchan began to shiver and rattle. Hands crossed over the chest and clutching his shoulders, he walked on behind Aliyar. He sustained himself on fantasies of Kesi and Ravi, like he had done for so long with Kallu in the rivulet, its malice and obscenity compounded with the lashing cold and darkness. Kuppu-Acchan tottered along and cursed.

'Round-head, shaven-scalp, good Muslim . . . .'

It was then that an unearthly voice spoke from the burial marshes:

'Stop!'

This was followed by a deep-throated chant.

'Who is that?' Aliyar asked.

'It is me . . . .'

'Oh, the Khazi?'

'Yes.'

In the faint light of an oil lamp they saw the Khazi's looming form. The Khazi held up his hand in caution, and said, 'Hush! There is a djinn here.'

Kuppu-Acchan froze.

'Be not afraid,' the Khazi reassured, 'just stand where you are, and do not swallow your saliva.'

Kuppu-Acchan did just that, he swallowed. All life drained away. After a little while the Khazi said, 'The Revered One has departed.'

Aliyar and the Khazi exchanged pleasantries. Kuppu-Acchan replied with funereal nods and grunts. When they had gone a little way, Kuppu-Acchan started to whine again.

'*Ya Allah*!' Aliyar swore. 'What is it this time?'

'Let me go home, beef-eating round-head, and pick up my blanket.'

'By then the fish will be asleep. We will have to wake them up.'

'I'll be back in a moment . . . .'

'Go, go, and cadge a drink from some sleeping bootlegger.'

Kuppu-Achan walked back home . . . . Kesi's door stood shut, but there were wide cracks in the wood. A small wick lamp dimly lit the room. Kuppu-Acchan peeped in, a long and bitter look. Ravi's torch and footwear were in the verandah. Kuppu-Acchan turned away and came to the bottle in which there still was much wash left. He drank in deep draughts, then picked up his old blanket, wrapped it round him, and set out to the Araby tank, aflame with intoxication and terror . . . . Aliyar was not at the spot where he had left him. He reasoned that Aliyar must have gone to the Araby tank all by himself.

When Kuppu-Acchan reached the tank, he realized that Aliyar had deserted him, abandoning him to the poothams and djinns. This was betrayal. Kuppu-Acchan called out into the night, 'O Aliyar! Where are you?' The night was climbing on to the evil hours; the kabandhas would soon be here to frolic in the tank.

'Ooooh Aliyaaaar!'

As if in reply, a wind blew in from the graves.

'Betrayer! Sinner!' Kuppu-Acchan began to cry; he wanted to get away, but the demons would be after him soon. Then he heard the bubbling noises of the fish at play. He faintly remembered something about fish curry.

Like a kabandha wrapped in a blanket, Kuppu Acchan edged towards the tank and stood gazing at the phosphorescent water. Silently he called out to the fish, and the fish heard him—a big-headed old denizen rose to the surface and swam towards him. Kuppu-Acchan leaned forward with the fish-trap. The bank he stood on was sodden. It gave way.

Kuppu-Acchan thought the skies had fallen all round him. The blanket sponged in the water and grew heavy like lead. He struggled long for breath and balance, and finally clambered to safety. Covered with the wet blanket and moss, Kuppu-Acchan sat on a rock like a kabandha and raised a great lament:

'Help me, somebody! I am dying!'

The Eastward Trail

THE NATIVES OF Khasak were not fond of travel, but the Pandarams were a visible exception. An immigrant community which had come in through the Palghat pass centuries ago, they were sworn to mendicancy and ascetic nomadism. Time diluted these observances; the Pandarams went back through the pass on their annual ritual pilgrimage. Clad in saffron, they were received with hospitality and reverence and given generous alms.

The Pandarams preserved some tokens of their history—the tuft of hair at the back of their heads, and the Tamil language which, mixed with the host language, resulted in hilarious oddities.

When on these pilgrimages, like the saffron they donned, they assumed new names as well—names taken from myth and legend—and acted like gods out of a long lost pantheon. The god-walk took half the year at the end of which the Pandarams came home to Khasak with their considerable earnings.

They had a secret skill which did not go well with holy mendicancy—trapping birds—in Khasak this caused no embarrassment. The wastes around Khasak were full of quail and partridge, and the holy mendicants spent the second half of the year living on bird meat and illicit toddy.

The Pandarams were great fabulists, because they had nomadic minds. They spun endless tales about the Tamil country while they waited in the liquor den for the quail to fry on the fire. In these tales the pilgrim progressed over unrelieved chalk-stone landscapes under a relentless sun, but at the end of a day's journey there was always a village, a woman, a god. Kuppu-Acchan joined the listeners sometimes, and even the mullah, to whet his profane curiosity.

Gopalu Panikker, the village astrologer and teacher of the alphabet, was an incongruous presence in a liquor den, and more so as he sat listening to an unlettered mendicant. However, Gopalu had time on his hands now, since the astrologer's teaching method found fewer takers with each passing day. The method belonged to the classical world; the children wrote out the letters on spreads of sand and chanted them in a dirge. They wrote with their forefingers on which they wore a dried gourd for protection. Eight long years of this unhurried ordeal, after which nothing short of decapitation could permit the scholar to regress on his phonemes. But the new school of the District Board made the child literate in a matter of months. Gopalu lamented in bleak prophecy, 'What learning is this? Our country is ruined!'

The country was of course Palghat, from whose fabulous metropolis barefoot kings had reigned over a twenty-mile radius in olden times. That once-sovereign country now chose to learn the alphabet in six months instead of eight gruelling years; Gopalu sensed the end of civilization. Those who sat in the den and listened to his words of doom—Kuppu-Acchan, the mullah and the bootlegger Mayandi himself—were sorry for the country and its uncorrupted province, Khasak. But Mayilvahana Pandaram was not unduly concerned. He was an itinerant, and if Khasak was doomed, there was always the country of his origin to go back to.

Gopalu had questions to ask, the questions squirmed within him, he couldn't voice all of them as that would amount to admitting to the collapse of the family's guild. Casting covetous eyes on the browning meat, Gopalu, vegetarian and pundit, asked, 'O Mendicant, what be the truth of your journeys?'

The truth unfolded in unending spectacle—villages over which gods stood guard, enormous terracotta gods painted bright against the austere rockscape. These gods came riding the East Wind and tapped awake the mendicant of Khasak.

'O Astrologer,' the Pandaram concluded, 'it is a call hard to resist.'

On many nights Gopalu listened to the wind; there were only the noises of palm frond, no god rode the wind for the distraught astrologer . . . .

Finally, he went to Palghat town to visit a fellow-astrologer to explore ways to restore the eight-year regimen to its old primacy. He stayed a week. When he came back home, he felt that something ominous had happened while he was away.

'Where is our son Ramankutty?' he asked.

Lakshmi his wife met him with stony silence.

'Has he joined the Board's school?' he persisted, 'Who got him enrolled?'

Not a word came from Lakshmi. Nor did she feel any guilt for what she had done when Gopalu was away. She had taken a step which brooked no turning back, she had taken the thimble off the child's deformed digit and stormed into the school. 'Maash,' she had told Ravi, 'teach him English. Make him a big man.'

She kept the image of the big man a desperate secret, hidden deep in her mind and memory—her town cousin Raghu Nandan who worked as a clerk in a government office. She wanted Ramankutty to matriculate in a suburban school and become a clerk like her elegant cousin. She wanted him to come home riding a Raleigh bicycle, wearing rimless glasses, a fragrant cigarette between his lips.

Intuition knows no secrecies; Gopalu Panikker confronted his wife, 'Tell me who gave you this advice, Raghu Nandan?'

Lakshmi began to sob. Now it was Gopalu's turn to be silent.

He did not pull the child out of school. The silence in the family lasted four days. On the fifth day he broke the silence when he bid farewell to his wife, 'Lakshmi, I shall return soon.'

He set out before dawn, his personal effects in a satchel, lighting his way with a palm-fibre torch. Lakshmi stood behind the gate, stood a long while, until both torch and traveller disappeared into the sunrise. 'O my tamarind goddess,' Lakshmi prayed, 'be with him.'

Nobody knew where Gopalu had disappeared to. Lakshmi gave perfunctory replies to queries, which nobody believed in any case.

'I can't see Gopalu returning in a hurry,' Kuppu-Acchan spoke from the load-rest. 'Not that it concerns me . . . .'

Aliyar heard this chance utterance and forgot it, but it came back in wild imaginings of catastrophe, in all of which the astrologer invariably perished. Gopalu owed the teashop a few rupees, this money would evaporate if those fantasies came true. So, slyly one evening, Aliyar chaperoned Lakshmi along the foot tracks unsolicited. 'O astrologer's wife,' he said, 'the good astrologer owed . . . .'

Lakshmi preempted Aliyar's proposition, 'You are not the only one,' she told him, 'he owes a lot of money to lots of people. I would have paid off everyone, O Aliyar, had I the money.'

When the mullah came to know of this he reprimanded Aliyar.

'I ought not to have done it, Mollakka,' Aliyar admitted.

'Put it down to Allah's credit.'

In the third month Gopalu returned under cover of night, and by midnight a cloud of subtle odours lay over Khasak. They rose from Lakshmi's kitchen. A fortnight, and Gopalu was gone again. And since Lakshmi was reticent, the others could not resist the temptation of the whispered word. Kuppu-Acchan quoted anonymous informants who claimed to have seen the astrologer work in the meanest of stations—as a butcher and pedlar of beef. Lakshmi ignored this purposeless malice, and walked about Khasak flaunting a necklet of gold with a pendant of phoney rubies.

The cattle broker Ramacchar was yet another exception to the inertia of Khasak; once every month he travelled to the Tamil town of Pollachi to trade in its famous cattle fair. He went by bus and barely managed to salvage the money spent on bus fare and food. The market was chaotic; countless animals were bought and sold, and in the dung and dust and whirling noise, the touts conned or terrorized, and snatched commissions from deals they had nothing to do with.

Ramacchar was an innocent tout; the deals he muddled that day left him penniless and famished in that alien town. It was then that he found himself face to face with the sage in saffron.

'O Astrologer!'

'Ha, Ramacchar, my countryman!'

Gopalu Pannikker embraced Ramacchar and took him to a teashop where he treated his fellow-countryman to the delights of Tamil cuisine—roasted malai patta and tea. Ramacchar listened to Gopalu's colourful story.

'I am widely respected here,' the astrologer said, 'for my healing spells.'

'The ones that wouldn't work in Khasak?' Ramacchar asked with a mischievous smile.

'True,' Gopalu said in the humility of success and contentment. 'Now let us go to where I stay. It is three miles away, can you walk?'

Ramacchar belched.

'O Astrologer, your roasted moth has given me wings.'

In a settlement three miles away from the market a gentlemen-farmer had given Gopalu half of his sprawling manor to use, for counselling and sorcery . . . . Gopalu cut short his work in the market, and with Ramacchar, set out homeward. On the way he cautioned the excited cattle tout, 'Rama, none of our old familiarity in the presence of my patron. A little discretion . . . .'

Ramacchar took on an obsequious stoop as he trailed behind the saffron-clad one . . . . Gopalu walked into the farmhouse chanting mantras. He introduced Ramacchar to his host, 'My old disciple Ramananda . . . .' The farmer greeted them with folded hands and words of reverential welcome.

'Your Master has been of great help to us,' the farmer said. 'He has rid this village of many evil spirits.'

Ramacchar, now Ramananda, bowed, 'His spells are mighty. There are many more spirits to be exorcised, I presume?'

'Indeed there are, holy one.'

The astrologer and the cattle tout lay down for the night, but neither slept, so they talked into the small hours. It was thus that Gopalu heard of his daughter's illness.

'It was typhoid, O Astrologer. She has recovered beautifully.'

'Did she suffer much, Ramacchar?'

'I hate to say it, but she did.'

Ramacchar told Gopalu how Kuttadan the oracle treated little Rukmini with his spells and later the mullah with Muslim spells, yet the fever raged. Then Ravi went all the way to the township of Kozhanasseri for those colourful capsules . . . .

'Ravi who?' Gopalu asked. 'The Maash?'

'Yes.'

What wandering, what weariness! The clay wick lamp thinned away. Gopalu thought of the children, the women and the withered elders; Khasak lay in the far reaches of the night.

'O Astrologer, have you gone to sleep?'

'No, Ramacchar.'

At that moment Ramacchar felt a tide of goodness rise and reach out to the astrologer's sorrow.

'I am finished,' Ramacchar said and broke down. 'I could strike no deal and I have spent my last copper. Save me, O Astrologer!'

It was thus that Ramacchar the cattle tout became Gopalu's fellow-sorcerer. On the first day at the manor, Ramacchar rose early and bathed and smeared with sacred ash he went into the audience room.

Gopalu, who came in a little later, was amazed. Ramacchar had put up a mighty montage of fetishes—fish bone, tortoise shell, betel leaves, red hibiscus flowers, many kinds of grain.

'Who taught you all this?' Gopalu asked in a whisper.

'Your grace, O Astrologer!'

And they waited for custom. A dozen or so people came for trivial fortune-telling, the collection was modest. In the afternoon a Tamil woman came with a difficult request. Her husband had left her for a mistress, could the great sorcerer of Khasak concoct a love potion which would bring him back? Gopalu looked in disdain at the neat wad of notes the woman had set down at his feet. He cast the cowrie shells to divine the future, desperate about the present, helplessly listening to his fellow-sorcerer improvise mantras and compose a litany of conjecture.

Gopalu put the cowrie shells back, and addresed the woman. 'We see a way out. Come back to us after three sunrises.' The woman was gone. Gopalu sat distracted and looked up at the parodist standing beside him. 'She wants a love physic,' Gopalu said. 'What shall I give her? Cartwheel grease?'

After the profanity of parody came a prayer; Gopalu poured out a ladleful of honey into a copper dish, he kept his hands on the dish and prayed to no god but to Khasak which breathed recovery into people; in that mute and wordless prayer Gopalu saw little Rukmni, the pallor still on her face. He had consecrated the potion with the sorcery of caring and sorrow.

He would give it to the woman when she came for the love potion.

Misfitting Phonemes

KUTTADAN, THE ORACLE of the goddess Nallamma, sat basking by the brook. He saw Gopalu Panikker's son Ramankutty moving suspiciously among the screw pine bushes. He walked over to the boy, and made conversation, 'Is your father back from the Tamil country?'

'Yes,' replied Ramankutty.

Kuttadan could see the boy's caginess.

'A pooja, is it?'

'Well, nothing really . . . .'

'Why then the lizard? Aren't you hunting one?'

An eight-year-old, even if he is a sorcerer's son, cannot keep a secret too long. So Ramankutty came out with the story, which Gopalu did not want revealed to the villagers prematurely.

'One of those ghosts,' said Ramankutty.

'Oh—'

'It has entered a man. A rich man.'

'A man from the Tamil country?'

'Yes. And he has a rich mill and a car.'

Something rose inside the oracle, something fluid and angry and tangible, like rancid palm brew, it exploded inside opaque memories. Overcoming it, Kuttadan said, 'That is good news. So let us get a big one. There . . . .'

On a tree stump sat a fat lizard in all his regalia, a scion of the vanished saurians.

'Let us get him, Ramankutty!'

'Stay, fat-head!'

'Charge!'

When the assault came from two sides, the lizard nodded his crested head and began clambering off the tree stump. Kuttadan cast his upper cloth like a net and caught the slow-moving creature. He secured it in Ramankutty's cloth bag and said, 'Tell your father it is a gift from me.'

'A real big one,' Ramankutty said gratefully, 'like a crocodile.'

The sorcerer's son went home, and Kuttadan climbed down the bank for a bath. The water was pleasantly warm. After the bath Kuttadan went to the mud-walled shrine of his goddess and sat before her grotesque image. It was in this chaste hungering, day after day, that he had worshipped her for ten celibate years . . . . As he sat before her that day a single thought spiralled through his mind: people come from far away to see Gopalu Panikker.

'Read this, dullard!'

Kuttadan heard the the voice of his dead teacher Rama Panikker.

Kuttadan could read letter after letter but he could never join them to build a word. Rama Panikker had not spared the rod, but it had only added to Kuttadan's stupefaction.

One afternoon, pursued by disjointed skeletal letters, Kuttadan was walking past Rama Panikker's house. It was in the yard of this house that the letters were taught in the morning. Lakshmi, the teacher's daughter, was standing at the gate, sunning herself after her bath, the fragrant paste of sandalwood on her bare breasts, tiny in pubescence. She had smiled at Kuttadan.

'Shall I teach you?' she had asked.

The more he wrestled with words to fashion a response, the more uncouth they became, 'We? Alone, together?'

'Yes,' Lakshmi had said, her smile still serene. 'There is no one at home.'

He had followed her into a room that smelt of decaying palm-leaf texts. She had made him sit beside her and written out the letters for him. The dismal veil was on him again, and he had failed to comprehend word and letter together. Lakshmi had sought to punish him. Nimbly she had parted his mundu and let her foraging fingers loose on his thighs. Then she had begun pinching him. It had hurt, yet he had wanted her to pinch him the more.

'Angry?' she had asked.

'No.'

'Where is it? Let me see . . . .'

She had parted his mundu again, hungrily spotting the red crescents on his flesh, feeling them, counting them playfully.

'Will you tell anyone about this?' Lakshmi had asked.

'No.'

He had given up words and letters for good then. He had turned away from script to the mysterious unbounded sound, to the voice of his goddess that rumbled inside his unknowing self. Since then he had passed by that gate many times. Lakshmi had always been there sunning herself, but she had showed no sign of recognition. There was something he wanted to tell her, but even as the words formed the phonemes slipped away.

Lakshmi became Gopalu's wife . . . . A rich miller from far away was coming to Gopalu to be exorcised.

'*Vango! Vango!*' Gopalu Panikker welcomed the miller in

Tamil to put him at ease. The swarthy giant from the Tamil country looked cowed by the evil spirit that was inside him. Gopalu comforted him and seated him on a mat. It was the dark quarter of the night before moonrise. Cicadas and an assortment of insects drummed the night into muted unrest.

The miller and the astrologer sat down to eat. The miller looked greedily on Lakshmi's wrist and palm as she ladled out rice and curries: the women of Palghat were bought off by rich Tamil men for their form and light complexion. The miller had heard about them, he had also heard about the sorcery of Khasak, about its cantos both black and benign.

Midnight. A tiny tongue of wild fire sprang to life on Chetali's slope.

'Good omen,' Ramananda said.

'*Shambho Mahatman*,' Gopalu chanted in undertones, '*Sayed Mian Sheikh*!'

Gopalu, Ramananda and the miller made their way to the funeral marshes. At a signal from Gopalu, Ramananda began to call out to little gods and friendly demons, an insane invocation, coupled with dire threats to the spirit that possessed the miller. Gopalu waded into chest-high funereal vegetation beyond which were the renuncient grounds garlanded with bone and plastered with ancestral ash.

Ramananda had softened the miller with generous draughts of liquor and blinded and choked him with incense. Ramananda walked farther over the dried bank of the marsh and waited for the final command from the great sorcerer.

'Go!' said Gopalu.

Ramananda bent down and cast the offending spirit into exile. At that very moment the miller saw a small flame light up on the bank of the marsh. The miller looked on amazed at the exorcised spirit burning away as it fled.

The sorcerers and the miller left; a lone man rose like the truth from the marsh where he had lain hidden. It was Kuttadan the oracle. He picked up the lizard, that morning's catch, and gently uncoiled the strip of half-burnt cloth from its charred tail. The oracle peered into the eyes of the lizard, into its ancient riddles. For one stupefying moment he thought it was not the lizard he saw but the transmigrant spirit. He did not want it to live, he strangled it.

Kuttadan stood on the marsh of death a long while holding the dead lizard. Then he felt that inexplicable effervescence inside his head again. He was seized with a wild desire to chase the miller and confront him with the lizard. But the next instant, the effervescence gave way to moonlight and mist—he saw the fine muslin and the red hibiscus. He felt the fingernails imprinting the little red crescents on his thighs.

'Did it hurt? Will you tell anyone?'

The seal of secrecy on the unjoinable phonemes!

Kuttadan flung the little corpse into the night. It landed amid the mould and marsh of a million endings.

The Festival

AFTER THAT NIGHT, the night of the burning lizard, Kuttadan locked himself inside the shrine. He sat in blind and fierce tapas before Nallamma, the goddess of smallpox. News of this penance spread in Khasak and soon to the villages beyond the paddies. On the seventh day Kuttadan flung open the door of the shrine and came out upon Khasak with oracular cries. He smote his head with the curved sword of the goddess. Oracles did smite their heads in frenzy and infliction, but the cuts seldom went deep. What Khasak now witnessed was not just ritual: the sword left yawning gashes across the scalp and blood clotted on the oracle's matted hair . . . . In the days that followed Kuttadan did not cease chastising his flesh. He walked over a bed of live cinders.

'Truly,' said the witnesses, 'the Sheikh has blessed him. Now we shall hear the Devi who has possessed him.'

Kuttadan's frenzy abated, but painful like the sword's edge, scorching like the fire-bed, one insistent memory pursued him, blotting every other. There, amidst the abysmal bafflement of the phonemes stood the girl after her bath, the pavu mundu round her waist, the red underclothing showing through the diaphanous wrap like a hibiscus flower. In the lunacy of his penance he wrapped the mundu around the goddess's waist. He prayed until the red hibiscus blossomed beneath her granite navel.

Kuttadan's little temple grew out of dereliction into a place of trance and prophecy. The goddess spoke through her oracle two days every week, sometimes oftener . . . .

On a Sunday after breakfast, Ravi reclined in an easy chair. He was at peace, and into that stillness came noises from far away, the cry of pain, of ecstasy, as the sword cleaved the flesh. The rhythmic clangour of bronze anklets blended with the oracle's cry. Ravi listened with rapt attention, and the cry sounded even more distant as he listened, as though the sword of the oracle was calling him to an unknown wilderness for cleansing and baptism.

That evening he told Madhavan Nair, 'Let us go to Kuttadan's shrine. Say, the coming Sunday?'

'To hear the oracle?'

'Well, yes.'

Madhavan Nair smiled and was curious.

'But why, Maash?'

Why was he going to the shrine, Ravi asked himself, why to a little hole in which stood a weird idol? Ravi sensed a great love welling within him. Devi, Ravi despaired, why have you chosen this lowly incarnation? Had she sought refuge from her own awesome cosmic self in the womb of Khasak? He thought to himself he was her kin, and would discover their twinhood in this intimate sanctuary. Then would he share his sorrow with her, the placental sorrow, generation after generation; as he thought this, the sorrow spilled over to become the sorrow of karma, it was the scar of the sinner, the orphan's pining, the despair of the one who thirsted for knowledge.

Ravi never made that pilgrimage.

'Poor Kuttadan has come by money at last,' Madhavan Nair observed on one of their strolls through the fields.

'Then his goddess must be real,' said Ravi.

Devotees from Khasak were soon outnumbered by those who came from outside. There were offerings in kind to be managed, accounts to be kept. Kuttadan acquired a handyman, Theinagan, who had once worked with the timber-thieves on the mountains . . . .

One day, after a whole crowd of migrant canal-diggers had visited the shrine, put money into the hundis and gone, Kuttadan sat cross-legged in the shrine and pondered over many things.

'We are no longer a little shrine,' he spoke to Theinagan with great solemnity.

'True, O Oracle.'

'We are a temple. We must have an annual festival.'

'We must, O Oracle.'

The core of the festival consisted of the mounted dancers, masked men in Kathakali costumes wearing enormous tinsel crowns, carried atop bamboo platforms on which they stood grimacing and yelling. There would be pipes and drums, and fireworks in the evening. At midday there would be a slaughter of chickens and a display of oracular frenzy.

The day of the festival arrived. Ribbons hung over the Mosque of the King and Maimoona's shop-front, garlands decorated the slender neck of Madhavan Nair's Singer sewing machine. By late forenoon a crowd had gathered in the central square, idlers from the nearby villages, and of course the grateful canal-diggers. Pedlars wove through the crowd, rustic toy-makers, sellers of cheap and abrasive cosmetics, women with trayfuls of knick-knacks. Both the mullah and the Khazi came to the shrine and burnt incense sticks. All was set for the festival, for the goddess to lead her oracle to the heart of Khasak.

Inside the shrine, Kuttadan donned the scarlet saree of the warrior goddess who would descend on him at any moment now. The worshippers would not be allowed to get too close to the shrine at such a time, but Madhavan Nair sought to have a word with the oracle.

'The venerable tailor, Nair, seeks the Bhagavati's blessing,' Theinagan whispered, conveying Madhavan Nair's request.

'What might be his affliction?' the goddess enquired.

'He waits outside.'

'Ask him to come in.'

Madhavan Nair entered and bowed.

'What is it, Venerable Nair?' the goddess asked.

'It is for the Maash that I come, O Mighty Goddess.'

'We are pleased,' the goddess said, now fully come into Kuttadan's mortal frame, 'the Maash can come.'

'I shall bring him when the frenzy mounts . . . .'

'Yes, that is better. And let the world know that great people seek Bhagavati's protection.'

Madhavan Nair left. Theinagan peeped in again.

'O mighty goddess,' he said, 'they are townsfolk. The frenzy must be spectacular, so that more schoolmasters will come to your altar.'

'Of course they will come.'

Now Theinagan was caught between two worlds.

'Yesterday,' he said, 'the oracle's mortal frame was troubled by a headache. We should not let that happen today. I have brought an offering of illicit brew, it is Chatthelan's very personal blend.'

'The Bhagavati needs no such stimulation.'

'Of course, Mighty Mother.'

The goddess grew thoughtful. 'What about the sulphate?' came the query from the other world. 'We presume the old sinner has not blended it with too much manure.'

'Just the right mix, O Mighty Goddess.'

Theinagan brought in pots filled with the chemical that cheers.

'Keep it there in the corner,' came the command, 'and let the dancers partake of it, and those that carry the dancing platforms.'

Kuttadan himself drank generously, and found it good.

The dancers came in their regalia, crowns on their heads, crowns firmly fixed with twine and gum. They entered the shrine one behind the other, drank in haste and in large quantities and left. The oracle's mortal frame sat cross-legged on a wooden stool, the mortal brain ratiocinated, the wayward phonemes, the diaphanous mundu, the crescent marks, the occult lizard. Soon the regressing mortal habit passed. Outside, a giant cracker exploded, and the goddess reponded with the oracular roar, 'Aaaaaaahhhh!'

The outcaste dancers replied from atop their platforms, 'Hooyyah!'

The festival began. Theinagan peeped in again and, raising his voice over the drums, supplementing speech with grimacing lips, said, 'The Maash is coming.'

The oracle's mortal frame stamped the ground, the bronze anklets clanged, the cry of the oracle resounded from the shrine again. The crowd waited, breathless. But something unforeseen was happening—the manifest goddess, as she cried out again, was also mysteriously making her presence felt on mortal innards. Kuttadan stood leaning on the sword, his legs striving in vain to twine round each other, like a woman in travail. Theinagan could see that the oracle was trying to say something, but the phonemes were lost in eddies of pain. A slimy serpent was coursing through his guts, the miraculous creature of the sulphate. In demented syllables the oracle gave Theinagan the message to be communicated to the crowd, 'No manifestation—Bhagavati—angry—tell—'

Theinagan raced out with the precious words: 'There is no festival, the goddess is angry!'

The crowd was in tumultuous disarray, all the platforms were down on the ground and the dancers squatted on them more dead than alive, abandoning themselves to their own helpless mess and stench. No one heard Theinagan's precious words. Three crowned dancers were racing towards the fields, chased by dogs. O Mighty Goddess, Theinagan lamented, why have you undone us? As though in reply, a noise rose from his innards, the conch call of the avenging goddess; he pressed his palms hard on his stomach, but nothing could stop the cosmic deluge. Theinagan too followed the dancers, running for the fields.

The men and women had gone, and so had the dogs. Ravi stood, looking out towards the screw pine bushes where Appu-Kili hunted his dragonflies. Behind the bushes crouched the dancers, he could see only their tinsel crowns as they glittered in the sun.

Scent of the Flower

RAVI LAY AWAKE the next morning. The gruesome comedy of the festival came back to him in a tide of disgust—the shame of men squatting to defecate behind scant cover, their tinsel crowns glittering above the bushes. Soon these became images of sadness. On their usual walk that evening Madhavan Nair told Ravi, 'You haven't heard the whole story, Maash. It was Kuppu-Acchan's dirty work. He got Chatthelan to put in a lot more of that sulphate than the guts could stand. The poor bootlegger innocently went along without realizing that the drink would become an instant purgative.'

'God!' said Ravi, 'Why did Kuppu-Acchan have to do it?'

'His idea of a practical joke.'

Ravi walked beside the tailor in silence. He had seen a celestial war, the undoing of a goddess.

'I want to visit the oracle,' Ravi spoke after that silence, 'this Sunday.'

'After all that has happened, Maash?'

'Yes.'

What strange ways this young man has, Madhavan Nair thought . . . . Sunday was three days away; Ravi kept those days to himself. He walked the sunsets all alone, and saw the gods of Khasak in the twilight. They stood guard over the follies of men. He saw them in the cavernous interior of the mosque, in the luminous breath of the mouldering dead, on the great tamarind tree, inside the serpent statuettes, beside tracks. What was the mystery they guarded? The palm grove that stretched without end, the twilight neither sunrise nor sunset could resolve? Perhaps this was his sin and his divinity, and the gods and goddesses its witnesses.

Sunday. As Ravi and Madhavan Nair set out from the school, Appu-Kili followed them.

'Why do you want to come, Kili?' Madhavan Nair discouraged their ward.

'Go catch dragonflies, Kili,' said Ravi more softly.

Appu-Kili did not smile as was his wont. He looked dejectedly in the direction of Kuttadan's shrine.

'It's all right,' Ravi gave in. 'Come along with us, Kili.'

The shrine was deserted. Kuttadan was nowhere to be seen, though it was the hour of the frenzy. A red-crested rooster strutted about in the yard over the accumulated trash. The door of the shrine was ajar. Ravi turned to Kuttadan's house. The freshly thatched palm fronds hid much of the verandah. Ravi bent beneath the fronds to peep in. There on the glazed mud floor sat Kuttadan's aged mother.

'Where is the oracle?' Ravi asked. Madhavan Nair repeated the question a little louder.

Slowly she turned an unseeing gaze on them, wrinkles radiating from twin foci of cataract. Appu-Kili was uneasy. He said, 'Etto, let us go!'

'Shhhh!' Madhavan Nair silenced him. Appu-Kili groaned.

'There, there!' the tailor cried out. The oracle, hiding all this while in a pit behind the house, sprang up and ran across the yard. He carried the curved ritual sword. Ravi and Madhavan Nair stepped aside. Kuttadan gave an oracle's cry, 'Haaaarchhhh!'

The crested rooster flapped himself up to the roof and crowed in alarm. Kuttadan began to smite his head; Nallamma, queen of the viral hosts, had seeped out of the idol and possessed the body of her oracle.

'Parighatam!' Kuttadan raged, *'Parighatam!'*

Parighatam, the corrupt form of *parihasam*, mockery! The oracle took a fistful of sacred ash from the shrine and flung it on Ravi. Ravi broke into a cold sweat. The frenzy ended, Kuttadan entered the shrine and bolted himself in.

Back in the seedling house, Ravi felt his heart beat faster. Madhavan Nair helped him to the easy chair, and stood near him in some anxiety.

'Better?' the tailor asked.

Ravi smiled.

'One of those passing fits,' he said.

Ravi rested and was soon well again.

'I'm thirsty,' he said, 'for water and air. I need a walk.'

'Do you feel well enough to walk?'

'I'm fine.'

The two walked past the lotus pond and over the ridge, they crossed the rail track of the east-bound train. Beyond the rail track was a grove where, on aged mango branches, owls dreamed and nodded; and further down, the teak forests. Monkeys, a whole clan, were crushing tender shoots of the teak into a red paste which they smeared on their faces . . . . From an elevation Ravi looked down. A picturesque village nestled amid the foothills.

'What place is this, Madhavan Nair?'

'Never suspected it was there, did you, Maash?'

'These hills do spring surprises.'

They climbed down to the painted valley.

'This village has no name, Maash. It is a fugitive place.'

At the entrance to the settlement stood a derelict shrine. Madhavan Nair gave the door a gentle push, a panel fell to the ground.

'My poor dear god,' he said, 'the termites are upon you!'

Smoke rose from one of the huts, from a pit of fire in the front yard over which bubbled a big vat of rancid wash. A sturdy, middle-aged woman stood stoking the fire. Madhavan Nair called out from the bamboo gate, 'We are parched—give us something to wet our throats.'

'Won't you come in and sit down, Venerable Nair?'

Ravi and Madhavan Nair seated themselves on little mats.

'I shall be there in a moment,' she said, and gave the wash a final stirring. She lifted the vat off the fire and set it down to cool. Sweat glistened on her bare breasts and trickled down their cleft. She trotted off into the back of her hut, and returned with a bottle of arrack and two cracked china vases.

'It is fresh,' she said, 'almost warm.'

'And what do you have to go with it? My friend here is the Maash of our new school,' and then Madhavan Nair went on to introduce her to Ravi, 'She is Kodacchi, the old faithful.' Kodacchi gave the newcomer a special smile of welcome, and asked Madhavan Nair, 'Would he like dried goat's gut?'

Ravi looked at Madhavan Nair helplessly.

'He finds it barbarous, my girl,' Madhavan Nair told her, and to Ravi, 'You'll enjoy it, Maash.'

Kodacchi produced a yard-length and roasted it over the fire.

'Delicious,' said Madhavan Nair savouring a piece.

'When is your husband coming back from the Tamil country?' Madhavan Nair resumed the conversation.

A two-year-old child began crying inside the hut; soon it crawled out and peeped at them in alarm. Kodacchi picked it up and pressed her breast into its mouth to keep it quiet.

'He may come back in two months,' she said, 'maybe in a month. He has taken a good measure of the black stuff to sell this time.'

'He goes over the mountain, Maash,' Madhavan Nair said with generous admiration, 'and dopes half the Tamil country. What do you do with all the money he brings in, Kodacchi?'

Her eyes glinted with rustic coquetry. 'I never see it anyway.'

No one moved or spoke in the other huts . . . .

The sun was setting when Ravi woke out of a sleep heavy as that caused by an opiate. A strange scent permeated the room, fetid and sensual, like rotting chrysanthemums. The mat smelled of the flower, and so did the woman lying beside him. He mopped the scented sweat from the brown spread of her body.

'Are you feverish, Kodacchi?'

Maybe not a fever, he thought, but the warmth of the body's arousal. Her flushed face was pressed close to his, it blotted out the sky and the menacing dusk . . . . Ravi heard the whistle of trains, the dull clatter of rails; it was the journey again. Into its great weariness dissolved the hut, the woman and her infant child. In the far valleys the spirits of evil danced round the unclean dead. Their bronze anklets clanged to the rhythm of the oracle's curse: *Parighatam! Parighatam!*

The sleep again, and the strange waking. He felt cold crystals all over his body. He tried to touch them but the effort brought on searing pain.

He saw a bangled hand extend towards his face and

pour a soothing fluid into his eyes. He could not see anything more, vision was lost in an arc of darkness above. Now he lay resting his head on her lap. He counted the floating husks of the Kalpaka.

Ravi groaned, 'Ma!'

'Do not move,' she said.

Slowly the eyes cleared, wet and cold. Ravi saw Maimoona seated beside his mat.

'Where am I?'

'In the Mosque of the King,' she said.

A bicycle bell sounded outside. Someone was leaning a bicycle against a wall. Someone was carrying a load into the room.

'Nizam-Annan,' Maimoona said.

'Tender coconuts,' the Khazi said, coming in, 'Let him have one right away, Maimoona.'

'Tender coconuts?' Ravi asked.

'Lots of them. Help you to get well soon.'

The sound of drums came from the heart of the village, and the prayer, the frenzied cry to the goddess of smallpox, '*Deviye, Ammae*!'

The crystals, dreaded pustules, burst. The oozing pus was the goddess' sacrament. It was from this sacrament that the scent rose, the scent of chrysanthemums blossoming in the night.

The Dalliance

CHRYSANTHEMUMS. THEY BLOSSOMED EVERYWHERE, in Khasak, in Koomankavu, in the valley of Chetali; the wind bore their heavy scent. The pariahs carried away the unclean dead, they hobbled in insane glee beneath the weight of dripping corpses.

'Let us hear what the astrologer has to say—'

'The signs are benevolent. Devi is pleased—'

'Let us hear our dear Khazi—'

'The pustules have sprung in the right places—'

'*Deviye, Ammae*!'

Ravi heard these snatches of conversation. He scanned the images, part real, part dream. He saw the faces encircling him—Maimoona, Madhavan Nair, the Khazi, Gopalu Panikker. There were others, but the curtain fell before he could put the pieces together. Now he was dreaming of the journey—the delirious return from the fugitive village, a walk like that of the Devas who walked without touching the earth.

The wind carried in the sound of ritual drums far away; the drums died down, Ravi was bathed in sweat. Someone was wiping the sweat away, strong hands over him, his father! He is better, he heard his father say, the fever has come down.

He was asleep again, now he was on his evening walk holding on to his father's little finger playfully. Along the tracks of sunset purple, the coffee bushes are afire with twilight.

See the little bird there, son?

Yes, Father.

He is the tailor bird. Do you see his little house?

Yes, Father. A house of sewn leaves.

As they walk away Ravi asks, Do the tailor birds' eggs have spots, Father?

Little blue spots.

He thinks of the little blue spots, and is amused. He nestles like a fledgeling against his mother's belly. She caresses his eyelids, My little star, she says, do you know whose these eyes are?

Whose, Ma?

Papa's.

And my nose, Ma?

Mamma's.

And the eyebrows?

Papa's.

The ears?

Mamma's and Papa's.

Mother scoops him up in a rejoicing embrace. As she sets out on her last grand journey into the noontide mirage, she gives him this message—all this is your precious inheritance.

Then the redemption of death, and the curse of rebirth.

Chittamma, he says, are you crying?

I cannot face it, she says.

The sin?

It is like dying.

Ravi kisses her on her downy upper lip. He asks her what remorse is.

There, over there, she says, listen.

It is the sound of his father's wheezing as he lies paralysed and asleep.

Ravi looks out of the window, the moon has risen over the valley, its light upon the coffee plants. Ravi remembers his walks among those plants.

Chittamma, he says, let me go to my room.

She bars his way. Ravi tells her sternly, Put on your clothes.

Then the farewell. His forehead pressed against father's feet, softly, without waking him, Ravi utters a silent prayer, Father who gave me these eyebrows and these eyes. I give up this nest of sewn leaves, I journey again. Bless my path.

'The rain has saved our Maash,' Ravi heard someone say, 'now the pustules will subside.'

'Merciful goddess!'

The fever was gone, Ravi felt curiously weightless. There were tiny stabs of pain when he turned on his mat and crushed the pustules prematurely . . . . In another seven days Ravi was well enough to speak.

'Maash,' Madhavan Nair said on his morning visit, 'you have received the Devi's grace. I can't believe you are getting well so soon.'

Ravi smiled.

'Did you see the tender coconuts my uncle has sent you?' Madhavan Nair asked.

'He has sent a whole plantation. Does it mean a pardon?'

Madhavan Nair laughed. 'Far from it,' he said. 'The war has entered another plane. He is angry with the Muslims for keeping you in a mosque! I asked him, where else? He is just angry with the Muslims.'

'Your uncle is crazy. A crazy old man with a heart of gold.'

When the pustules erupted on Ravi it was Sivaraman Nair who found Ravi's plight distressing and wanted him moved to a home where he could be looked after. There was something else that worried the landlord as it did the others; the summer recess had begun early because of the epidemic, the children stayed home caught in the enveloping terror, and if Ravi lay in the seedling house any longer, the splendrous phantoms of the epidemic would linger on and scare the children away from the school altogether. Sivaraman Nair found it hard to locate a willing host for the ailing master; it was when they sat round and despaired that the Khazi burst upon them in anger and said, 'The Maeshter will stay with me. In my haunted home!'

The village was one vast flower-bed. Nallamma strung garlands of pus and death, she raised bowers of deadly chrysanthemums; the men of Khasak saw her and lusted, the disease became a searing pleasure in which they haemorrhaged and perished. Little children died as she suckled them in monstrous motherhood.

Ravi was well on his way to recovery. One day as Maimoona stooped over him to drop breast milk into his eyes, he said, 'A little later, Maimoona. I'm sorry I make you do these intimate jobs.'

'It is Janaki's breast milk, not mine.'

They laughed.

'But I'm really worried that you move so close. What if you catch the disease?'

'I have got Nizam-Annan's talisman round my waist.' She continued, her voice wavering, 'I also got myself vaccinated.'

'Have many others got vaccinated too?'

'Yes, a good many. Shame you didn't. What kind of school maeshtar are you.'

'I wanted to experience death.'

'There is time ahead of you, all the time you need for many deaths. Now let me drop the milk into your eyes.'

'Wait . . . .'

Maimoona held back the dropper.

'What are you looking at?' she asked.

'Your hands,' Ravi said, 'I would have hated to see them scarred.'

Maimoona rolled up her sleeves as far as they would go. Ravi gazed on the blue filigree of veins.

'Why do you stare so hard?' She was petulant.

'I was looking at those blue veins.'

'You shouldn't. While this disease is on you, Nallamma is your mistress. And she is a very jealous one.'

The scabs began to fall. Ravi was ready for his first bath. The Khazi prayed, the mullah sent the gram and the medicinal turmeric and neem paste to be used in place of soap. Madhavan Nair took charge of the bathing.

'I didn't want to tell you all this while,' the tailor said, 'Kuttadan . . . .'

For some reason Ravi knew what was coming.

'Is he gone, Madhavan Nair?'

'Yes, Maash.'

'The goddess has been harsh.'

Madhavan Nair paused as he poured warm water over Ravi. He said, 'I wouldn't say so. She granted him lasting love.'

Madhavan Nair recounted other tragedies. Kuppu-Acchan had lost his eyes—those two sentinels of fiction and scandal were now pits of blood, Devi's crushed crystals. There would no longer be the bird of gossip perched on the load-rest, no more the sarus crane gazing bewildered at the sky reflected in the shallow water.

Ravi had seven baths and the last trace of the disease was washed away. Yet he stayed on in the haunted mosque. The Khazi moved to another ruined mosque. The days wore on. The epidemic was in retreat, dragging its last victims along . . . .

One noon Ravi lay listening to the summer wind as it blew cleansed and free through Khasak. He took out a bottle of potent arrack hidden in a corner.

'Shall I pour some for you, Maimoona?'

'Chi! Chi!' She turned her face away.

As Ravi took a sip, Maimoona looked on, concerned.

'I am not ill any more,' Ravi said.

'But this spirit is deadly,' she said.

He took another sip. 'How is the mullah?'

'He wants very much to see you, but his big toe hurts, and it is marshy and slippery here . . . .'

'The toe? Where the sandal pinched?'

'Yes. Nizam-Annan has gone to Kozhanasseri to get medicine.'

The liquor seeped down like a slow, soft fire.

'Maimoona,' Ravi said, 'those blue veins—'

He paused awkwardly. Maimoona rolled up her sleeves playfully.

'Isn't that dress too tight? For summer?'

She did not reply. She rose to go.

'Stay on,' he said.

'No. I must go!'

'It is hot outside . . . .'

She walked down to the Araby tank; Ravi lay in the cool of the mosque and let his gaze wander over the tank and the wastes beyond, haunted places which the villagers still avoided. He witnessed Maimoona's bath in the haunted waters . . . . In the potent quiet of the noon, Maimoona came back to the mosque, her clothes washed and wet, drying on her body. Ravi pointed to a clothesline inside the room. One by one, she took her wet clothes off and hung them on the line to dry. When she had put all of them away, she turned round and stood before Ravi. He saw the blue veins spread delicately from arm to shoulder, from thigh to navel. The Khazi's talisman hung from a black thread round her waist. Ravi held the talisman between his fingers.

'No harm will come to me,' she said, 'as long as it is round my waist.'

With a smile Ravi undid the knot. She did not resist as he put the talisman away. She looked dreamily at her clothes on the clothesline and said, 'It is just a month after you illness. I wonder if it is all right—'

It was late afternoon when both of them got up. There was still some arrack left, Ravi held out the bottle for her. She sucked in noisy and eager mouthfuls. As she turned to go she reminded him, 'Take care of yourself.'

Peace descended on Ravi; he was now the helpless infant god, afloat on the deluge, lying on a pipal leaf, the Creator forever beginning his sorrows anew.

The Song of the Sheikh

CHAND UMMA CAME to the Mosque of the King where Ravi was convalescing. Ravi looked at her scarred face; he said, 'You shouldn't have come. I can see you need more rest.'

'Allah did not will it,' she said. 'I could not come when you needed me.'

Both fell silent. Then Ravi asked, 'How are the children?'

Chand Umma broke into convulsive sobs.

Ravi sat up, full of anxiety.

'My Kunhu Nooru, my son—' she spoke through her sobs.

'Chand Umma!'

'My son is not well at all.'

Ravi took his first unsteady walk to the village that morning, to Chand Umma's house . . . . Kunhu Nooru and Chandu Mutthu lay on frayed durrees spread on the floor.

'Anno!' Chandu Mutthu greeted Ravi, irrepressible as ever. 'Salam!'

'Salam, little one!'

A wind swept down and the thatch shook, the brittle fronds rose and fell like ticks on a wheezing dog. Ravi knelt beside Kunhu Nooru and felt his forehead. A low fever simmered. The pustules had drawn themselves inward, into the inner body. Where the pustules had been, there was now a dull red rash like flower-beds on distant hillsides, deceptive and deadly.

'Kunhu Nooru!' Ravi called to him. A feeble smile flickered across the boy's face. He was hidden far away behind the smile, a distant listener inside a mysterious fortress.

A gleaming blue fly flew in with a loud drone; it brought no happy tidings. It flew round Kunhu Nooru in wide circles. Chand Umma looked at this droning messenger, aghast. Like her child's eruptions, she withdrew into herself. Ravi had brought oranges for the children; as she peeled an orange she felt that the fruit and her fingers were an unfathomable distance away.

Chandu Mutthu remembered the chocolate.

'Anno,' she asked, 'will you bring some more?'

'I shall,' Ravi said.

'With silver paper?'

'Yes, my little one.'

Kunhu Nooru died that night. Chand Umma told Chandu Mutthu that Ravi had taken her brother to the seedling house.

'Umma,' asked the little one, 'has the boy got well?'

'Yes, my precious.'

'Now he will grow big, won't be, Umma?'

Chand Umma went to her backyard. She slammed her forehead on the trunk of a papaya tree, flew at the tree again and again, demented. There was no pain, there were no tears. She came back into the house, her eyes glinting with anger. She sat beside Chandu Mutthu. She sat waiting.

Two days later Chandu Mutthu told her mother, 'Look at me, Umma. I am well, am I not, Umma?'

Chand Umma took her child's tiny palms into her own and looked long at her face. The pustules had grown inwards. The wily, haemorrhagic malady. On the child's face and neck, arms and shoulders, barely visible, lay the sovereign rash.

'Who brought the oranges, Umma?' asked Chandu Mutthu in a feeble voice.

'Maeshtar-Annan.'

'Will he bring chocolates?'

'He will, my little one.'

'With silver paper, Umma?'

'With silver paper.'

'Umma—'

'What is it, my child?'

'In the yard, Umma—'

'What, my precious?'

'The boy has come, Umma. He is calling me out to play.' Then she looked into the night and said, 'Boy, get that big black dog out of my way.'

At midnight the villagers heard it, the song of the Sheikh's chosen insane: *'I shall take you in my arms. I shall not give you up to the yawning earth!'*

Allah-Pitcha, sleepless because of his sore toe, sat up and listened. Thithi Bi said, 'It is the Wandering Fakir!'

The Wandering Fakir, Chand Umma's father, had fled the curse of the tamarind goddess. His milk-white beard reaching down to his waist, the dust and bruises of many roads on his feet, he went past the sleeping homes and shops of Khasak. He stood on a crest of rock and looked towards the house of his blemished daughter . . . .

A din of voices awakened Ravi in the morning: aged men pleading aloud, women wailing. Madhavan Nair came to the mosque soon after.

'If you feel you can walk,' he said, 'come with me, Maash.'

'What is the noise, Madhavan Nair?'

'Chandu Mutthu is dead.'

'Madhavan Nair,' said Ravi sitting back on his bed, 'rest yourself.'

The words came out of him inspired, full of the poise of death. Ravi lit the stove and put the kettle on.

'Let us have some tea first, Madhavan Nair.'

'You are wise, Maash. There is no use racing with death.'

They drank their tea unhurriedly, and set out to Chand Umma's house.

The crowd had dispersed. One group was over the ridge, headed for Chetali, raising peasant war cries. The Muslim elder, Ponthu Rawuthar, stood guard at Chand Umma's gate.

'Ponthu Rawuthar Anno, what is happening?' Madhavan Nair asked the elder.

'I do not understand, Madhavan. I do not.'

Aliyar came up to them and said, 'Come with us!'

Ravi and Madhavan Nair fell in with the last stragglers moving towards the mountain. Those who led the crowd called out, cupping their palms around their mouths, 'Give us the mayyat, fakir! Give us the body!'

When they had covered some distance, they caught sight of the Wandering Fakir. He walked a hundred yards ahead, a wild, enormous man carrying Chandu Mutthu's little corpse in his hands.

'O Fakir . . .'

When the chasing crowd got closer, the fakir shot stones at them from his sling.

'Give it up, Fakir! Give us the dead body!'

The stones deterred the crowd. Madhavan Nair stopped and stepped aside.

'Maash,' he said, 'the ancient one has got me.'

Blood showed, a cosmetic dot on the forehead; soon it became a trickle.

Ravi mopped it with his kerchief.

'God should have spared us this gruesome scene, Maash.'

The early sun worked on Ravi like a hallucinogen.

'Madhavan Nair,' Ravi said. 'hold me!'

Ravi spun round losing balance. He held on to an Arali tree. His eyes darkened, he retched and threw up the undigested tea and bile.

Ravi sat down in the shade of the Arali tree.

Madhavan Nair stooped over his friend.

'Better, Maash?'

'Let us go back.'

They plodded back to the village.

Far away the cry still sounded faintly, 'The body! The body!'

The fakir threatened to throw a spell on his pursuers. That slowed down the crowd, and finally sent it back dispirited.

The fakir climbed on to the Sheikh's mazar. He laid down the beloved body amid the minarets of rock. He sat beside it and sang a lullaby of death. Anyone who dared intrude was met with stones from the sling. The wake lasted five nights. On the sixth day it was Appu-Kili who came down the mountain.

The villagers went up. The Fakir was gone. Chandu Mutthu lay there, a puddle of melting flesh beside the crypt of the Sheikh.

That afternoon Ravi, escorted by Madhavan Nair,

returned to the seedling house. Appu-Kili accompanied them.

Looking at his ward the tailor said, 'O Valmiki, saint of the anthill! Go to the brook and wash. There are termites crawling all over you.'

When Ravi entered the seedling house, he felt he had strayed through many births to reach this haven once again. The book half-read, the ink bottle, the shaving set, the teapot and cups—everything was where he had left it.

A subtle scent pervaded the room, the gentle incense of the traveller. It was the journey of things unmoving and inert, a journey through time. As he wiped the dust and aired the room, he was sad that he had disrupted an incredible pilgrimage.

The Conversion

AND SUMMER WAS over; dew glistened again on the morning grass of Khasak. The school reopened.

Ravi glanced through the register lying in front of him, he had underlined some names in green—the names of those who wouldn't be coming to school anymore: Vavar, Noorjehan, Uniparathy, Kinnari, Karuvu. He had only underlined the names, he couldn't bring himself to cross them out. Like the fakir who kept his dead grandchild on the mountain and would not give her up to the grave-digger, Ravi kept the names. The lines of green became the little windows of his temple through which he gazed, listless. Outside, sun and dew, grass and palmyra, in repetition and rebirth, in endless becoming, sorrowless and without desire . . . .

Ravi looked up from the register at the places where the dead children used to sit. He did not call the roll that day.

During the epidemic Appu-Kili had gone off to the mountains where his hair had grown long and matted. He came back to school with lice multiplying in its knots. The lice grazed about and at times herds of them crawled out in search of other heads.

Ravi was teaching history and he thought the example would come in handy.

'The Aryans came in exactly this manner,' he told the children. 'They came driving their herds of cattle looking for fresh pastures.'

The matter of the lice did not stop with history. That evening Cholayumma, Kunhamina's mother, had given her a bath and was dressing her hair with scented oils when a louse jumped out.

'Where did that louse come from?' Cholayumma asked.

'That was Appu-Kili's louse, mother,' Kunhamina said. 'It must have come like the Aryans.'

'What are you blabbering about, child?'

Kunhamina told Cholayumma the story of the Aryans. It did not impress her. The next day Cholayumma complained to Ravi. Appu's knotted locks must be shaved off, that was the only way to get rid of the lice. Ravi had no desire of offend the Parrot. So he asked Madhavan Nair to put the proposition to him as gently as possible. Surprisingly the Parrot agreed without resistance . . . . When Appu-Kili got to the barber's shop one of the mendicants was having his head shaved leaving a tuft at the back.

'Shall I give you such a tuft, O Parrot?' the Hindu barber asked in passing.

'See mine,' encouraged the mendicant. 'Do you know what—if you keep one they will give you their daughters to wed.'

The Parrot turned on his timeless grin, 'Get a girl?' He told the barber, 'I wan a tuff.'

And when the Parrot was leaving tonsured, save the tuft dangling behind him, the barber gave him this advice, 'If ever you fall off a tree, pull yourself up by the tuft.'

Appu-Kili stood before Madhavan Nair, the grin still on his face.

'Look at me, Madhavan-Etto!'

Madhavan Nair was angry at first, he disliked anyone having a joke at the Parrot's expense, but he couldn't hold out for long against its charming absurdity. Matters of destiny, he said to himself.

'Ayyo! My Parrot!' he said. 'One needs the thousand eyes of Inderjeet to see you!'

The next day there was chaos in the school. It became difficult to restrain children wanting to decorate the tuft with flowers and berries and silver paper. Only Kunhamina kept away—she was sad that her mother and the louse had brought all this on Kili.

Ravi was writing out a sum on the blackboard; when he turned round, he found Kunhamina in a state of distraction.

'What is it now, my little one?'

She did not respond.

'Tell me,' Ravi said again.

She began tentatively, 'Oh, Saar . . . .'

Ravi waited. Kunhamina found the words at last, 'Do lice have souls, Saar?'

He paused, then said, 'If we have souls . . . .'

'We have, Saar.'

'Then, I suppose, so do lice.'

Ramankutty interceded, 'Lice do have souls, Saar.' That decided the matter because he was the sorcerer's son.

Kunhamina wanted to know more, 'What will Appu's lice be in their next lives?'

Will they be reborn as lice? Or will they return as people or wild elephants and whales or little microbes? Ravi's mind suddenly went back to the jasmine-scented night when he had taken leave of his father in silence and stealth. Will you, my father, come back to me in another birth, if you have sins to wipe out? And who does not sin? Will you come back to me as the creature I detest most? There on the wall it clung, its eight legs stretched, looking at him with eyes of crystal in love and uncomprehending grief. He crushed a piece of paper into a ball and threw it at the spider. The spider ran around in wild circles, and again came to its mindless trance on the wall. Ravi swatted it with his sandal. It stayed on the wall, a patch of broken limbs and slime and fur. Ravi stood a long while in contemplation. Gratitude welled up inside him, the gratitude of procreated generations. He shivered and the sandal fell from his hand. What an offering to dead ancestors, what a shraddha!

And now he turned to Kunhamina's question, 'Frankly, my little one. I don't have the answer.'

But the children had the answer. They knew that those who went away had to come back, and Vavar, Noorjehan, Uniparathy, Kinnari and Karuvu would be fair babies again. They told Ravi the legends of Khasak, of those who had come back from the far empty spaces, of the goddess on the tamarind tree, of Khasak's ancestors who, their birth cycles ended, rose again to receive the offerings of their progeny; then like the figurines on the throne of Vikrama who narrated the idylls of the King, each child told Ravi a story:

Kunjuvella was the daughter of Nagan the toddy-tapper and Thayamma. When she was five they had gone to visit their relatives in Koomankavu. While there Kunjuvella had died. The same year in Koomankavu, Kannamma, the wife of Ayyavu, had given birth to a daughter. They had called her Devaki. Even as a little child Devaki would spend hours gazing vacantly recalling something real and inscrutable. Kannamma would put the child on her lap and ask, 'What is the matter, my child, that you sit and brood?' The child would say, 'I am thinking, mother.' On her fifth birthday she had told Kannamma, 'Mother, I have another mother.' Kannamma had not taken much notice of this. Five-year-olds knew no limit to fantasy. But Devaki had kept insisting and weeping. She had wanted to see her other mother. She had led the way and the family had come to the house of Nagan and Thayamma. 'That's my house,' Devaki had cried out from the gate. She had recognized every nook and corner. She had found an old peashooter hidden away in the attic and had rejoiced at the sight of her old plaything. 'Mother,' she had asked Thayamma, 'where is father?'

Thayamma had wept. She had stretched her hands across the awesome void to hold this child of hers. 'Father has gone,' she had said, 'he fell from the palm tree.' The watching women had wiped their tears; Devaki had not understood, wasn't hers a simple home-coming?

She had asked Kannamma, 'Mother, don't you remember that day at the pool?'

Kannamma had asked, 'Which day?'

'That day, that day, many days ago when you were bathing, didn't I come to you on pattering feet?'

Memories had come back to Kannamma. She had remembered bathing in the pool at sunset, and a funeral procession passing by. That was five years and ten months ago . . . . As Devaki had grown up these memories had weakened, soon they were lost altogether in profane and worldly torrents.

Two days after Appu-Kili began to wear his tuft there was a Muslim festival. Muslim children, their heads shaven and scented, appeared in joyous and colourful crowds before the mosque. Appu-Kili would never miss a festival.

'Hey, Parrot!' the Muslims greeted him, 'But what is this handle at the back of your head?'

'Get a girl,' the Parrot grinned.

'*Yaa Allah*! What have the Hindus done to your head?' the Muslim boys said, 'Surely the mendicants are the culprits. With a tuft like that you will become a mendicant and that is not the surest way to get a girl.'

The Parrot stood bewildered, yet smiling.

'Shave it off,' the Muslim said, 'shave your head clean.'

'Get a girl?'

'What have we been telling you all this while? You just shave that knot off and go ask Maimoona Akka to marry you.'

The Parrot grinned until his cheeks disappeared. The Muslim children took him by the hand and led him to the Muslim barber. When the tuft was shaved off, one of them said, 'Now that it has gone this far and he is going to marry Maimoona Akka, why not convert him? How about it?'

'Of course,' the Muslim barber agreed.

The tuft vanished in a few strokes, and freed at last from pagan connections, the Parrot walked out grinning. Somebody brought a frayed fez cap and put it on Appu-Kili's head.

In the evening Ravi had just lighted the lamp and got into bed to read when Maimoona stormed into the room.

'Both master and pupils are becoming riotous,' she said.

'What happened?'

'Keep that lunatic under control.'

'Which lunatic?'

'That Parrot of yours!'

Ravi shut his book and sat up. While he was raising the wick, she said, hiding her charm beneath her anger, 'I won't speak to you again.'

Madhavan Nair came in as she was leaving.

'What did the houri come for, Maash?'

'Something about the Parrot. We'll find out tomorrow.'

Madhavan Nair sat at the foot of the bed.

'Haven't you heard it, Maash? The Parrot has been converted.'

'My God! Into what?'

'Need you ask? The Fourth Way, Islam.'

Through the window the Parrot jumped in, the fez cap on his head . . . .

The next day Sivaraman Nair walked through Khasak in great agitation. 'Have the infidels gone this far?' He coughed and stumbled, he stood before the school and called out, 'Maash, this is not good. There is still something called Hindu civilization. That cannot be shaved off.'

'But Sivaraman Nair,' Ravi tried to calm him, 'was it any of my doing?'

'But this is definitely not good. You mustn't be led astray by that Madhavan. He is the one who has disgraced the family. He is a Communist.'

At the foot of the big banyan tree in the square of Khasak, the people were merrily discussing the Parrot's choice of religions. Massaging his feet with oil the mullah argued that once a convert, neither man nor parrot had the right to go back. The Khazi declared, 'We will go by the majority.'

The majority was yet to make known its decision. Appu-Kili sat in the front row of the class wearing the frayed fez cap. As a Muslim they had given him a new name—Appu-Rawuthar. Ravi did not call Appu's name while calling the roll. He decided to wait until he knew the majority's verdict.

Sivaraman Nair wrote out a long petition to the School Inspector. Ravi was creating religious strife in Khasak, leading minors astray. He concluded the letter with words picked out of an old petition: *For which act of kindness it is my bounden duty ever to pray.*

Within a few days the panchayat's verdict was known. The Parrot was to be allowed the freedom of both religions. For certain days of the week he could be a Muslim. For the rest he could be a Hindu. If necessary Hindu, Muslim and Parrot all at the same time.

When months passed and Appu's fez wore thin, when his hair grew long and matted, the lice were born there again. They came pattering on little feet. Vavar, Noorjehan, Uniparathy, Kinnari, Karuvu and all. Their fathers and mothers did not know them. Among the karmic wefts of hair, they sat grieving and waiting.

Ravi lay down to sleep. Through the window, the sky shone and shivered. Oh God, to be spared this knowing, to sleep. To lay one's head down, to rest from birth to birth, as forest, as shade, as earth, as sky . . . . The knowing eyes grew heavy, the lids began to close. Leaving their skies the stars descended on the screw pines to become the fireflies of Khasak. Out of these infinities a drizzle of mercy fell on his sleep and baptized him.

The Cry of the Muezzin

EARLY THAT MORNING the Khazi came to the seedling house. Ravi was awake in bed.

'Maeshtar!'

'Come, come, Khazi.'

'A matter of some urgency,' said the Khazi without stepping in. 'Can you spare five rupees?'

'Certainly.'

Ravi got up and took out the money. He did not ask what the money was for, the Khazi volunteered the information, 'We are taking Mollakka to Palghat. To the hospital.'

Ravi remembered seeing the mullah two days ago in the fields, much to his own embarrassment—the priest was squatting behind the screw pine bushes to ease himself. He had looked helpless, his eyes dull like old porcelain . . . . Now Ravi asked the Khazi, 'The lesion where the sandal pinched?'

'The same lesion, Maeshtar. It will not go.'

'Sit down, my friend. I shall come along with you. But let me make some tea.'

'We can save time if we went over to Aliyar's instead.'

So they had a hurried breakfast at the teashop.

'Sivaraman Nair has spared his bullock cart,' Aliyar informed. 'It is ready.'

Ravi and the Khazi were soon on their way to the mullah's house.

'Who cooks for you now?' the Khazi asked Ravi, remembering the tea Ravi had offered to make.

'I do it myself,' said Ravi.

'Poor Chand Umma! What a curse!'

'Surely the curse must end some time.'

'The gods are often more unwise than men.'

Sivaraman Nair's bullock cart stood waiting in the mullah's yard.

'He has sent us his best bullocks,' the Khazi observed.

Ravi had been to the mullah's house before, but only now did he fully feel the poignancy of its decay . . . . The mullah lay on a mat, his toe bandaged with oil-soaked rags. Ravi sat down beside him and stroked his forehead.

'We will pray that you get well soon, Mollakka,' Ravi said.

A smile flickered across the face of the priest.

Thithi Bi spoke from behind the half-closed door, 'This is what the old sandal has done.'

'True,' Ravi reassured her, 'it is a shoe-pinch. Nothing to worry about.'

Even as he uttered the words, Ravi realized the lesion had been on the toe for many months. The Khazi undid the crude bandage, Ravi saw the bloodless and quiescent lesion the size of a silver rupee.

'Does it hurt?' Ravi asked the Khazi.

'It doesn't.'

'It is the poison of the leather.' Thithi Bi said, wanting to believe her own words. The mullah groaned.

'Don't hesitate, Umma,' Ravi said, 'if there is anything I can do . . . .'

Thithi Bi choked. She said, 'You have been generous, Saar. He never tires of talking about you.'

The Khazi reached out to a shelf on the wall and took down a bottle of medicine. With much effort the mullah sat up, leaning on the Khazi, and drank the bitter concoction like an ailing child. He turned for a moment to look at the Khazi in grateful reminiscence . . . .

The cart returned at dusk, homing in on the village over the parched fields, tossing its hood as it climbed on to the square. There was a small crowd in front of Aliyar's teashop—Madhavan Nair, Gopalu Panikker, Ponthu Rawuthar and some others. Madhavan Nair waved the cart to a halt, Sivaraman Nair's fast bullocks reared their heads and panted.

'Where is the mullah?' the tailor asked.

Getting down from the cart the Khazi answered, 'We have put him in the hospital.'

'What did the doctor say?' Aliyar asked.

'He will medicate and watch, and then tell us.'

'Accursed footwear!' the outcaste Malli said in dismay.

'Cursed indeed. It grew fangs like the hamadryad.'

'The snake dwells in our sandals and our belts.'

'Even our fingernails can become the fangs of the snake.'

'Truly said.'

The mullah had been in the hospital for ten days now. Thithi Bi had moved to Palghat; she joined the many squatters on the verandah of the ward, keeping vigil day and night, snatching moments of fitful sleep leaning on the thin pillars.

Sunday. Ravi and Madhavan Nair set out for Palghat town. They found the mullah better. He could sit up, he could speak a little. Ravi held his hands, the mullah smiled.

'Mollakka,' Ravi said, 'I have brought oranges.'

The mullah smiled again, the smile of a stranger.

'I have no desire, Kutti,' he said.

The smell of disinfectant canopied the ward like the scent of many flowers. Beneath it waited the weary travellers into the unknown. They did not know one another, they exchanged the obscure farewells of strangers.

'I will be well in a week,' the mullah said.

'You surely will,' Madhavan Nair encouraged him. 'It is the work of an ill-fitting sandal after all.'

As they took their leave the mullah held them a little while longer—he needed to speak. Who was sweeping and cleaning the school? Ravi tried to put him at ease. But the mullah spoke on, each syllable drawn out painfully. He had taken wages and had not worked, but he would make amends, he would be back in a fortnight. Until then Ravi should ask Ponthu Rawuthar's daughter Rokkamma to come and sweep. He must tell her it was the mullah's word. Exhausted, the priest sank back. The mask of the stranger was back on and his face receded into the enchanted distance. The wages, reckoned across this void, became a karmic debt.

Outside the ward Ravi and Madhavan Nair spoke to the doctor. It confirmed what Ravi had suspected. The doctor told them that a tissue sample had been sent to the big hospital in Vellore for pathological examination, and nothing could be said until the result was known, but malignancy was a fair guess.

Ravi and Madhavan Nair got off the bus at Koomankavu and began the walk home . . . . Far away from Khasak, medicine men trained their all-seeing scanners on a cell of the mullah, the cell was an entity, a planet of the microcosm, it had its own aeons of time, and life sprouting on its land and in its water. This was cancer, the needless violation of inert surfaces. Even as the two of them walked along the winding footpath, through the palm groves and across rivulets, the earth-cell rejected the violation, and the cosmic toe twitched in deceptive, painless malignancy.

They were nearing Khasak.

'Maash,' Madhavan Nair asked, 'what is this illness?'

'Existence, civilization- –'

'Surely, you are not jesting?'

'No.'

'What is the remedy?'

Ashahado Anna la Ilaha Illallah wa
Ashahado Anna Mohammadur Rasoolallah.

The muezzin's cry!

'Who is that, Madhavan Nair?'

'The Khazi.'

Hayya Alas Salat
Hayya Alal Falah
Alla ho Akbar
Alla ho Akbar

Nizam Ali was making the prayer call for Alla-pitcha after seven years of estrangement.

The Mask of the Stranger

THE MUEZZIN'S CRY subsided in Ravi's dhyana, he now hearkened with his inner ear:

There is no God but the Omnipotent One
Come to this tabernacle and worship Him!

Ravi thought of Khasak's house of prayer, the sad brooding mosque, its attic breeding bats and vermin, and its mullah silenced by a dreaded disease; Ravi heard anguished generations of priests calling to worshippers. The gravestones kept no count, they softened and crumbled over men changing to mould and marsh. Ravi could not sleep, he rose restless. He looked out: a dull moon lit the mist, the last of the ferries were torching through the night.

Ravi got out and walked into the sleeping village. He knocked on the tailor's door. Madhavan Nair opened the door and then tottered back to bed.

'Get up!' said Ravi.

Madhavan Nair rubbed his eyes, yawned and smiled.

'You, Maash?' he said. 'What is the time like?'

'It is just eleven. And I am thirsty.'

'I have nothing left.'

'Then let us wake the bootleggers.'

Madhavan Nair tilted the earthen jar in the corner for a

cupful of water and doused his eyes and forehead.

'Is this journey necessary, Maash?'

'Come, let us go.'

'To the bootlegger?'

'Not straightaway. Let's go to your uncle's.'

'My uncle's?

'I want to go to bed with that cousin of yours, the cousin you didn't make.'

Madhavan Nair laughed, a brief and bitter laugh. He said, 'She is all yours.'

'I am sorry, brother.'

They held hands and walked like children to Chathelan's distillery and home. From a bare ten feet away came the sound of heavy breathing. Ravi fancied entwined and sweating bodies, he was swamped by the onrush of the images of sin.

'O Chathelan!' Madhavan Nair called out. The bodies disentangled themselves, the billowing breath fell into a softer rhythm.

'Who is that?' Chathelan's woman asked.

A chimney lamp lit up in the verandah dispelling the deep-breathing mystery, and soon Chathelan came out of the hut.

'Sorry, Chathelan, our Maash wants a drink.'

Chathelan was evasive—there was a bottle of freshly distilled arrack, but it was for the Village Officer.

'Come on, Chathelan,' Madhavan Nair coaxed the bootlegger, 'the Village Officer can wait. Here is a rupee over the price.'

'How can I deny the tailor and the teacher?' said Chathelan and went back to get the bottle.

As they walked away with the freshly distilled spirit Ravi suggested, 'Let us give Kuppu-Acchan a drink.'

'Should we, Maash?'

'Let us—'

'If you so desire—'

Kuppu-Acchan sat up on hearing the footfalls; he scanned the light with his pits of darkness and listened; 'It's us,' Madhavan Nair announced.

'Madhavan? Maash?'

'Yes.'

'Is the night far gone?'

It was a pleasantry, Ravi was aghast.

'Kuppu-Acchan,' Madhavan Nair said, 'we have brought a bottle of arrack. We would like you to share it with us.'

He smiled in the direction of the voices, and slowly felt his way to the door of the room where Kesi slept.

'Get up, my child—'

'Hai, hai! You won't let me sleep—'

Madhavan Nair lit a wick lamp in the room. Kesi had rolled off the mat onto the smooth floor, her bodice and mundu had slipped from their places.

'Kesi—'

'Hai, hai—'

The moon had set when they left the house, the wind had cleared the mist and the stars shone as in a luminous nightmare.

'Madhavan Nair, did you look at the old face?'

'It was sad.'

'Beyond the sadness—'

There was quite a quantity of the arrack left, and they decided to drink it beneath the palms.

'There was something on that face, Madhavan Nair. Sights that the blind can see . . .'

The roving eyes of blindness haunted Ravi, sockets of blood and rheum, the eyes of transcendent seeing. Faces surrounded him, each with its mark of indifference . . . . He remembered his journey to the ancestral village where his grandfather lived. The short walk from the road led him through picturesque countryside. Then, ahead of him, he had seen his grandfather on his morning walk. Ravi had hastened and overtaken him.

'Grandpa!'

The old man had stopped and turned slowly.

'Grandpa, it is me, Ravi.'

The old eyes had groped for focus, and over the slavering lips had spread the smile of an ancestor gone away.

What had that smile been, Ravi was destined to wonder during his desolate journeys. Was it love? Or the ennui of recurrent being which amused and distressed the baby in its cradle? Or was it the passion of the seaside vigil, the wait for the last wave? Ravi did not seek to violate the mystery, he was content to recognize the mask of the stranger . . . .

'Let us sit down here, Madhavan Nair.'

'Hand me the bottle, Maash.'

They sat on the moist grass and drank out of the bottle.

'Maash,' Madhavan Nair reminisced, 'it was here, amid these palms, when I was away studying Vedanta, that my mother played the harlot . . . .'

The east wind began to blow, it was past midnight. Khasak lay deep in sleep. Madhavan Nair went on, 'I went away when I was twenty-one. My mother was thirty-five, she had delivered me when she was just fourteen, and was widowed early . . . .'

She had not wanted him to go. She was young, looked younger than her years, and had a voluptuous body.

'If you leave me and go,' she had told him, 'I will be all alone.'

But Madhavan Nair could not find rest in that house. He resembled his father down to the finest detail—his mother had once said this in joy, but soon he found her saying it in resentment and fear. In their little hut he could find no sleep, nor could she . . . . When he came back after five years with his blind Guru, there were guests in the house, drunken and riotous. When those men were gone, his mother had taunted him, 'So you studied Vedanta, my son?'

Madhavan Nair thought of blind Kuppu-Acchan who had still not tired of seeing, and of his Guru to whom blindness had given the vision of peace. Madhavan Nair could not solve the puzzle, he was content with the day and night, he saw butterflies mating in the sunlight, he saw the rain, the brook, the mountain, he saw disrobed thighs vibrate with the rhythm of death. Each seen object drained away the meaning of seeing . . . . Ravi and Madhavan Nair were on a magic stairway to a house of sin when the cock crowed and the hour of enchantment ended. The stairway disappeared.

It was not yet dawn. Ravi rose and stood on unsteady legs in the palm grove. He saw the dark silhouette of the mosque far away. With his hands pressed against his temples, he bitterly called the muezzin's cry:

Allaho Akbar!
Allaho Akbar!

Madhavan Nair was asleep on the moist grass. Ravi looked round, the abodes of God and men had vanished, there were palms all round, only palms, which once yielded the brew of forgetting and bliss.

What was left in him was bile, the residue of prayer. Ravi bent forward and retched.

The Feast of the Ancestors

ONCE EVERY THREE or four years Khasak feasted its ancestors. Muslims and Hindus prayed and ate together. Then at night they congregated in the arid waste behind the mullah's mosque and talked about other worlds. They felt the presence of their beloved Sheikh, he walked along the pathways of Khasak communing with the ancestors. Four years had gone by since the last feast; the Khazi went into retreat in the Mosque of the King. The privileged few who had access to the mosque brought vivid accounts of austerities. On the fifth day of penance, a Sunday, the Khazi emerged intense and fevered, and ordained the fifteenth day from then as the day of the feast.

Khasak was astir. Frenzied troops of children came to the arid ground, they uprooted thorn bushes, they scared away the snakes with strong-scented tree barks. The animal to be slaughtered was chosen—Cholayumma's black goat, which she sold to the village for half the market price.

'But it is a eunuch,' said Ponthu Rawuthar the village elder, 'and can bring no luck.'

'So what?' retorted Aliyar, 'We have got him for half the price, and that is luck enough.'

Aliyar agreed to keep the goat till the slaughter, since

Kunhamina began crying over the animal as soon as Cholayumma told her that it was to be sacrificed. Aliyar came to Cholayumma's house and led the goat away. Let it be tethered to the load-rest, he decided, till the day of slaughter. Till then it would be his mascot.

The eunuch goat was a sweet-tempered animal, tame as a pet. Aliyar fed it dosas in the morning, and tea, which it drank in delicate sips. Mutthu Pandaram the mendicant asked Aliyar, 'The goat has a credit with you, does it?'

'Yes. And why not? If your cousin Karumandi Pandaram can have a credit here, the goat can have it as well.'

'What be the truth of that, O Aliyar?'

'Simple is the truth, O saffron-clad one. Your half-brother owes five rupees and a quarter for the buffalo meat he gobbled. He is on a pilgrimage, and I can get hold of neither the Pandaram nor the money.'

That goat soon became an attraction for the children. They slipped out of school to gather green shoots for it, and let out peals of laughter as the animal grazed their fingertips while nibbling greedily at the berries they held forth. Kunhamina kept away.

When the children left in the evening, Appu-Kili came to the goat. He brought it neither fruit nor flower, but only a cretin's love. He stroked its condemned neck, gently he pressed his head against the goat's and crooned consolations.

The Thursday before the feast the Khazi decided to go to the hospital and see the mullah.

'I shall watch him till Sunday morning.' he told Aliyar,

'and if he is well enough, I shall bring him in a bullock cart by midday.'

'Let him at least lie down before the fire of sacrifice,' Aliyar said. 'We could borrow the Maeshter's easy chair.'

'I go now, Aliyar. And keep some money for the rental on the cart when I return.'

The Khazi set out for Palghat town . . . . Maimoona bathed and smeared herself with scented oils, and walked the square displaying the Champaka flowers she wore in her hair. She came to the seedling house. Ravi had not got out of bed.

'Our teacher has too much sleep,' she said, walking in.

Ravi sat up yawning and looked round for cigarettes.

'Here—I have brought you two packets. Smoke away!'

Ravi took the packets, pulled out one and lit it.

'Again,' he said, 'you have brought me the Tiger brand. It is firewood.'

'It is the wood of the funeral pyre.'

As she said this, the cigarette burst into flame, and Maimoona looked on in amusement. Ravi spat it out and lit another.

'Teacher-Kutti,' she said, 'your innards will burn out.'

'Let them, no one will miss me when I go.'

She moved a pace closer, and said, 'A lie!'

'I am sorry, Maimoona.'

God, said Ravi, You gave me Your love, gave it with fond indulgence, yet it dies in the deserts within me. I am in flight, Merciful God: let me savour my weariness. Then through strange and wondrous Mandalas came the voice of his father: My beloved son, here I lie paralysed, awaiting your return.

Father, do not pine for me, said Ravi. I journey away to free us both from memory. I walk, an Avadhuta, a renunciate along the shores of the Infinite Ocean.

Journeying, I let my slough of memory moult away. When I reach the last shore, when I wait for the last redeeming wave . . . .

His father's voice said, I cannot die without my memories, death will be incomplete.

Ravi was back in gross reality. 'Maimoona,' he said, 'what news from Palghat?'

She shrugged her shoulders and said, 'No news.'

When the Khazi reached the hospital, he found Thithi Bi seated on the verandah of the ward, leaning on a pillar.

'Umma, how is he faring?' the Khazi asked her.

'Asleep.'

'Did the doctor tell you anything?'

'Nothing, my child.'

The doctor and nurse on their afternoon round undid the bandage. The lesion was still on the toe drained of blood, a cool and sanitized presence. The mullah lay in a daze. The Khazi suddenly came upon something moving on the bed, tiny as a paddy husk.

'Lice,' Thithi Bi said sadly.

'These lice are dangerous, Umma.'

Thithi Bi wiped her eyes. 'The doctor wanted the beard shaved,' she said, 'but Mollakka cannot let the beard go.'

Gently she stroked the old beard. The frazzled hair stood on beds of dandruff, the grey lice moved over the scaly crust, baffled and thirsty.

That afternoon the doctor called the Khazi out, and asked him, 'Are you a relative?'

'No, Saar, I am the Khazi of Sayed Mian Sheikh.'

'Who is that?'

'It is a spirit, Saar.'

'Very well,' the doctor said, 'since you are close to the

family, I shall tell you. It is cancer, and it is far gone. I suggest you take him back.'

The Khazi came back to Thithi Bi and said, 'These English medicines are no good, Umma. Let us go back.'

He did not stay on to hear what she had to say. He walked out of the hospital and past the fort of Tipu Sultan; behind the fort the land was deserted. The Khazi stood on a grassy mound and looked at the mountain pass far away, he heard the birds and the thunder of a distant train. He was agonized, ecstatic: Khasak's mullah was dying!

In the Mosque of the King. The early dark of its ancient interior. Cobwebs and dust.

'I feel like a housebreaker,' Ravi said. Maimoona did not say anything.

'Here is a drink for you,' he said, holding out the bottle towards her.

'How does it taste, Maimoona?'

'Warm, pleasureable.'

They lay down on an old mat. The night was a luminous blue over the gravestones.

Suddenly she tensed. 'Do you hear?' she asked. She rose naked from the silt of darkness.

'What?' Ravi asked.

It came through the lucid summer night:

La Ilaha Illallah!
La Ilaha Illallah!

'What is that?' Ravi asked again.

Maimoona said, 'The dead body.'

The Flowering

THE BUFFALO CART hired from Palghat lumbered over the rough track. Beneath its yoke hung the mullah's lantern. The Khazi walked in front, the lantern threw his shadow, black and serpentine. The cart came into the square and came to a halt before Aliyar's shop. Raising his hands the Khazi called in a resonant bass:

La Ilaha Illallah!

Soon the villagers' lanterns threw an arc of dull light around the cart. They closed in, their lanterns raised; the mullah lay in peace at last, his head on Thithi Bi's lap. The Khazi gestured to the crowd, 'Take down the mayyat.'

In the light of several lanterns the Khazi gazed again on the dead face. The lice had gone. The hair of the scraggly beard, brittle and silvery, continued to grow on their livid scabs in the macabre after-life. The lice knew the coming of death, like seers who sensed the advance of the distant hurricane or the earth tremor. On the journey back from the hospital, they fled the strands of hair, they raced down the precipices of facial wrinkles, then across the interminable desert of the cart's matting, and over the edge of the cart's frame plunged into the infinite void beyond.

The villagers turned towards Chetali with personal and inarticulate prayers.

The Mosque of the King; Ravi and Maimoona stood in its haunted darkness.

'Go,' said Maimoona, 'go!'

Ravi stood dazed by the perils of the walk.

'Go,' Maimoona repeated, 'go!'

Ravi stepped out, and over sharp quartz and slippery rock he walked towards the lanterns of Khasak. He turned to look back—Maimoona was bathing in the haunted waters of the Araby tank . . . . Ravi skirted the square and reached the seedling house.

The mullah's body lay in the mosque, awaiting burial the next morning, the day of the feast.

The women of the village sat round Thithi Bi, consoling her.

'It is fortunate,' Cholayumma said, 'being buried on the day of the sacred feast.'

'It is fortunate,' Thithi Bi agreed weakly.

'The Sheikh's mercy.'

'Yes. His mercy.'

After the burial the villagers went through the ritual bath to cleanse themselves for another encounter with death—the ancestors. Night fell, oil lamps shone on the consecrated ground, their flames as wild as the East Wind that blew over them. Drums beat the clip-clop of the ancient cavalcade. Tonight the mullah would walk with the ancestors.

The tattoo put Ravi to sleep, and dreams of peace came to him. He saw the mullah, now radiant, changing the litter in the school yard into flower-beds.

The epidemic had unsettled the work of the school. There

was an examination to go through, and the annual picnic. Then the summer vacation.

'What examination is this?' Madhavan Nair laughed. 'The same class, the same teacher.'

'Like human destiny, isn't it?' Ravi observed.

'A lot like it, Maash.'

'It is really misleading, Madhavan Nair. There are far too many classes in my school for any teacher to handle—'

Pupils concerned with the rebirth of lice, with journeys in time, with dinosaurs, pupils who taught their teacher the lessons of wondering and belief.

The day after the examination, in which the children shared the questions and answers, they gathered early for the picnic to Chetali. They set out with song and laughter. They crossed the big ridge and began the climb in the kindly sun. As they climbed higher they saw giant insects and plants with large leaves. The children broke ranks and went after these. Singing gave way to glad noises of discovery. Ravi kept anxious vigil as he brought up the rear of this disorderly column. Kunhamina walked beside him.

'Why have you children stopped singing?' Ravi asked them.

'These butterflies, Saar,' came the answer, 'so big, Saar!'

'And these red spiders, Saar, with silken coats!'

'And these dragonflies—'

Appu-Kili had declined to join the picnic. Perhaps the tutelage had ended, Ravi pondered in sadness, and the Parrot was about to embark on a new and solitary quest.

The children walked on chattering, squabbling. Someone had hurt a toe, another had stepped on a thorn.

'Why doesn't somebody sing?' Ravi suggested again.

The children prompted each other, nudging and

pinching. They were noisy again, when Mangustan the youngest began a solo song, a high pitched melody.

I utter the Bismi, my dear God, I have not forgotten the sacrifices and the offerings . . . .

The children knew the song.

'Saar,' said Kunhamina, almost in tears, 'Mollakka wrote this song and sang it.'

It was the ballad of the Badr War, it brought the Badrins to Khasak, the battle raged in the palm groves . . . . Ravi and the children were on the top of the mountain. They stood round the Sheikh's grave, the crypt guarded by minarets the millennial winds had carved out of natural rock.

At noon the class sat down to eat, they shared and ate together. After that it was time to play in the rocky pool of Chetali.

Adam told Ravi, 'There is a water demon in the pool, Saar!'

'Can we throw stones at it, Saar?' asked Mangustan.

'It comes up for air,' said Khadija, 'it changes form and flies out like a water fowl.'

'She doesn't know, Saar,' Kholusu said, 'it is a winged serpent, Saar!'

A winged serpent? The sunlight flooded Ravi's memory. A winged serpent with a diademed head, riding the mirage for a lonely child?

'Well, my children,' Ravi said, 'don't throw stones at the water demon. It is a gentle being.'

Ravi drew away from the children as they played in the pool. He sat beneath a Vaka tree which stood in full bloom. He was surprised to find that Kunhamina had followed him there.

'Don't you want to play in the pool?' Ravi asked.

'I feel . . .' she struggled with the word, 'shy.'

She came close.

'What is the matter with you?' Ravi asked, looking into her eyes.

'May I sit down, Saar? Near you?'

'What are you sad about, my little one?'

'Sadness.'

Ravi stretched out a soothing hand. Kunhamina collapsed over him, delicately. And then she was on his lap, heavy and mysterious.

'Go, little one,' Ravi said, 'join your friends.'

She rose, she walked away a few paces. She turned and came back.

'I am ill,' she said.

Her eyes brimmed over.

'Ayye!' Ravi said, 'crying?'

Kunhamina pressed her hands over her navel and bent forward. Ravi held her. Suddenly he saw them on the silver anklets and on her feet—crimson drops!

Ravi clenched and unclenched his palm, where the lines of fate lay like desert trails; the crimson drops had fallen on them.

Ravi gazed in amazement on the miracle, the first blood-flowers of womanhood!

The Peace of the Lake

RAVI'S MIND WENT back to the mountain and to the girl bent over him in intimacy and pain. What lay, Ravi wondered, between the loss of innocence and rites for departed ancestors.

The school closed for summer, but there was much paperwork to be done, work become burdensome through postponement. Almost every week there would be some routine query from the District Board on the strength of the school or on the level of literacy in the village. This had persuaded Kelu Menon the postman to visit Khasak every week. Kelu Menon, now grown old, chose Sundays for his weekly or bi-weekly visits, days when Ravi could spare time to talk to him. Ravi was the learned one and Kelu Menon took pleasure in conversing with the learned . . . . That Sunday, early forenoon, Ravi caught sight of the messenger coming over the big ridge. These walks, from village to village, were long and lonely, and were occasions for fantasy; Kelu Menon would jog along at times and imagine he was the mail runner from another time, a legendary hero with spear and bells and rucksack labelled 'Royal Mail.'

'At last, Maash!' Kelu Menon called out from the gate, 'You have a real letter this week. Not a brown envelope from the District Board!'

The postman dusted his feet, came in and made himself comfortable on one of the classroom benches. He began rummaging in his bag, 'I'm sure you have one. I can't tell its contents, it is in English. Ah, here it is!'

He handed Ravi the opened envelope. Ravi took the letter out, and began to read. The postman watched in mounting anxiety.

'All is well, Maash?'

'All's well.'

The delicate scrawl on classy parchment, the trusting message, and the imminence of it all, *Ravi, this is me . . . .*

'It is good news, isn't it?' Kelu Menon repeated.

'It is.'

'The Lord of Guruvayoor be praised!'

Ravi folded the exquisite blue parchment and slipped it back into the envelope. Kelu Menon, now at peace, settled down to gossip, 'It's elections in Kozhanasseri—to the panchayat.'

'I didn't know.'

'You sit here reading and teaching while things happen in the world outside. Kozhanasseri is all set to go red!'

'Interesting.'

'Do they know about it in Russia?'

'I suppose they do.'

'Oh yes. They have their spies.'

Kelu Menon got up and shifted his shoulder-bag into a more comfortable position.

'It's getting to be midday,' he said. 'Let me get on.'

Kelu Menon left. The winged serpents rose in the mirage and beckoned to Ravi with anxious passion.

Ravi took out the letter and read it again:

Ravi, this is me, your Padma. It was seven years ago that we lay on the cool sands watching the birds of night streak overhead. If I come again to disturb your peace, pardon me.

I will reach Palghat on the tenth of May. The train reaches Palghat early forenoon. Here in Coimbatore, I am Jyoti's guest. Remember shy little Jyoti, our classmate at Tambaram? He is District Collector here and has been of great help.

Wait for me.

Padma

Ravi looked at the signature, looked long, absorbed, at that image of the self; his own signature was in disuse, it might have worn away in his loneliness. Its spirit might migrate to the whorl on the thumb before the final dissolution. Padma, gazing at him from that pictogram, tenderly! He gazed back in arid gratitude.

Ten more days to go; Ravi was surprised to find that he was still capable of impatience.

'You look drawn, Maash,' Madhavan Nair observed on one of their walks. 'Must be the heat.'

'Must be—'

'Monsoon is going to be heavy.'

The usual gambits, repetitions.

The ten days were over. Ravi rose early, he saw the Morning Star shine down in cool brilliance. He walked to Koomankavu flashing the fibre torch. Then the first bus to Palghat . . . . He was early. After coffee at a wayside shop, Ravi climbed over to the platform. The platform wasn't crowded and at its ends there were trees and benches scented with coal and steam . . . . The train, a ricketty 'passenger', came in with the clatter of ancient pistons.

'Do you know me, stranger?'

'I don't.'

Ravi looked at the gorgeous silk she wore, at the thick glasses grown a good deal thicker, and then for a long while at the beaming face.

They held hands and moved towards the railway restaurant, and sat facing each other, too burdened to talk, hungrily, greedily, taking each other in.

'Come,' she said, 'some place where we could rest . . . .'

'I can't take you to my seedling house . . . .'

'Seedling house?'

'Where they used to stock seedlings before transplanting.'

'You live with them?'

'Yes. With a different kind of seedling.'

'Ooh, Ravi!'

'We could try the guest-house at the dam site.'

'Then let us go.'

In a cab, on the roads of Palghat town. The sullen pre-monsoon air heavy-laden with the damp. The sweat, the discomfort.

'You need to wash, Padma.'

'And you . . . .'

'I need more than a wash, I need a change of clothing.'

'Why didn't you bring some along?'

'There weren't any clothes back in the seedling house.'

'What do people wear back where you are?'

'Tree bark.'

'Let us buy something less fancy than tree bark. Shirts and dhotis.'

'I am stone broke.'

'We shall take care of that.'

'Okay. Buy me something in flaring red and green.

Something really loud and obscene.'

'Why?'

'Because the women back there will gasp in wonder.'

'Ooh, Ravi.'

They fell silent. Then Ravi spoke, 'Did I hurt you, Padma?'

'This world is full of hurts. The other world too, if there is one.'

'There is. That is what my pupils have taught me.'

The cab left the town behind. They were on the road to the dam. Deep-hued landscape. A lone bus grinding along, senile. A migrant tribal with beads on her bare breasts. A bulldozer, timid like a temple elephant, meekly giving way to a rattling cab . . . .

In the suite in the guest-house, Padma threw the window open. It looked out on the vast lake of the dam, sunny, scintillant and cool.

'Ravi!'

'Yes, Padma?'

'You didn't ask me about my bizarre search—for you.'

'I didn't.'

'Well, then I'm not going to tell you.'

'Oh, tell me.'

'Months of tedious investigation, that's how I closed in on your sanctuary. God! What is it called?'

'Khasak.'

'Yes, Khasak.'

In a Matth in Kashi, beset with lepers, in the sarais of Prayag, in the Quaker Centre in Madhya Pradesh; the trail threatened to fade ever so often. At last in Bodhananda's Ashrama. Meanwhile Jyoti had alerted the vast network of bureaucracy.

'In the Ashrama,' Padma said, 'a Swamini asked about you.'

'Did she?'

'Do you remember anyone called Nivedita?'

'Nivedita. I remember.'

'A stunner!'

Ravi smiled bitterly.

'Has America turned you lesbian?'

'I'm not going to tell you. Get the glasses.'

Ravi took the glasses out of a cupboard and placed them on the table.

'This is rather good whisky,' she said, 'I hope the prohibition cops don't worry us here.'

Ravi heard the metal cap crackle open. He broke the ice.

'Cheers, Ravi—for the Tambaram evenings!'

'Cheers, for the night birds in Luz!'

'I could cry . . . .'

'That'll be messy.'

Silence for a while.

'Bourbon on the rocks, as they say,' she said. 'Like it?'

'Not particularly. It isn't as good as our spirits.'

'Your spirits?'

'Yes. Khasak's moonshine.'

'Oh God, I could curse those spirits!'

Over the lake a cloud bank darkened, clouds the lake sent up and took back as its own rain. A catamaran sailed heavily over the lake towards the mountain.

'Ravi,' she said, 'don't you want to know what has happened to me?'

'I do.'

'I went to Princeton. Remember our guest at Tambaram?'

'I remember. And what did you do at Princeton?'

'Research. All these seven years.'

'Playing with prisms. Galileo's presumptuous lenses! . . . I gave up the Galilean search, at least for some time. And so began my search—for you!'

Ravi filled the glasses again.

'I went to your house in Ooty,' she said. 'They don't know where you are, Ravi. This is cruel.'

He was raising his glass, but put it back on the table.

'Tell me,' he said.

'I stayed there. I slept in your bed.'

Moonlight over the mountains, jasmine creepers outside the windows, creepers entwined like mating serpents.

'And then?'

'The next day I went out with your Chittamma for a swim.'

'Mmm.'

'We swam a lot. And, Ravi, what a beauty she is . . . Ravi, where are you?'

'I'm listening, Padma.'

'Your father is very ill. Ravi, do you want me to go on?'

'Go on, Padma.'

'The Luz evening. The letter you made me read. I have never forgotten his mention of the twilight. The twilight has consumed him.'

What is remorse, Ravi asked himself. The dying sunlight on distant palms, on the mountains. The wind was cool, the breeze from the lake.

'Ravi!'

'I'm listening.'

'Come away with me.'

A long silence. Sunset gave way to the early stars.

'I hate to say it, but he may not be with us for long. Plan something for the future. I have a job in Princeton. I can support you, and you can resume your studies where you left off.'

Ravi laughed.

'What studies, Padma? What research?'

'You mock me, Ravi. I hate this.'

A cry rose within her. And he spoke inside his own impenetrable silence—there is nothing to learn by looking at the galactic desert outside, turn the spectroscope inward, to where He has set his bow in the clouds within as a sign of the covenant between Him and the earth. Break the Galilean lenses—the Florentine was wrong, he tempted men with a finite calculus. The confessor and the inquisitor were right, for the earth is not round but an experience of the fallible human mind.

Ravi lay on his back, he lifted her over him and saw her breasts and waist paler than the rest of the sun-rich body.

'Ravi—'

'Yes, Padma—'

'Tell me you'll leave Khasak.'

With incredible lightness came the answer, 'I will!'

'Is that a promise?'

'It is.'

'And you'll come with me to Princeton . . .'

'I don't know, Padma.'

She began to sob. Ravi received her sorrow like a desert does the rain.

'What are you running away from, Ravi?' asked the despairing voice.

I wish to escape nothing, Ravi answered from within his silence, I want to be the sand of the desert, each grain of sand; I want to be the lake, each minute droplet. I want to be the laya, the dissolution.

The Journey Begins

GREAT CLOUDS DISSOLVED over Chetali. The monsoon swept over Khasak. In the pouring rain the School Inspector's peon came to the seedling house. The front door was locked. Appu-Kili sat cross-legged in the verandah, watching the rain water run down the eaves.

'Hey, you there—' the peon called out.

Appu-Kili neither saw nor heard, so deep was his absorption in the running water.

'What rudeness is this?' said the peon. He climbed on to the verandah and tapped the cretin with the tip of his umbrella. Appu-Kili leapt up, startled.

'Etto,' he lisped, 'aaa yoo a pootham?'

'Where is the Maeshtar?'

At the mention of the Master, Appu-Kili smiled soulfully and said, 'He gon catchin daagon fies.'

The peon turned away in a towering rage, and came to the square looking for the tailor.

'You insult me—' the peon said.

Insult the peon? Madhavan Nair was taken aback.

'I don't understand—' he said.

'I didn't mean you in particular. I meant the whole lot of you, the Maeshtar, and strange caretaker who made faces at me and called me a pootham.'

Madhavan Nair reconstructed the scene and in a moment fear of catastrophe cleared from his mind.

'O Peon,' he said laughing, 'that must have been our cretin Appu-Kili '

'I don't care who it was.'

'We shall make amends.'

'But tell me, O Tailor, where is the Maeshtar?'

'What is the matter?'

'First you tell me--where is the Maeshtar?'

Madhavan Nair stepped out of his shop, and said, 'Come, Peon-Saar. Let us go some place where we can sit and talk in comfort.'

In Aliyar's teashop, seated close to the hot samovar, he said, 'Tell me, O Peon, is something the matter?'

'Of course.'

'Tell me.'

'Where is the Maeshtar?'

'He is away for a few days.'

'Then let him find out for himself when he returns.'

'Aliyar,' Madhavan Nair said, 'Appams for our respected peon. And what do you have there? Steamed bananas—'

The peon ate and drank with relish. He softened.

'These youngsters,' he said, 'how they invite needless punishment.'

'Certainly you can tell us what the crime is,' Madhavan Nair said, 'whatever be the punishment. After all we live in neighbouring villages.'

The peon leaned forward and said in a hushed voice, 'There is a report lying with the Inspaetar Yajaman . . . .'

An anonymous letter, but one containing grave charges: *Ravi spends his time telling stories instead of teaching, his morals are unsound, he keeps a false admission register, he is fanning religious hatred, he spreads it with the help of a black magician named Nizam Ali.*

One more steamed banana, and the peon became still more communicative. The charges, if they weren't disproved soon, could cost Ravi his job, and might result in the school's closure.

A new inspector had taken over, a young and impetuous officer, one picked up after his tenth class as an inspector-trainee. Beneath his severe exterior he was kind and helpful, and appreciative of good food and the good life.

'What kind of good food?' the tailor asked hiding his disgust.

'Chicken—'

'Would he like quail and partridge? The Pandarams will massacre a whole flight of wild birds, if we just give them the signal.'

The peon made obscene noises, chewing the birds in anticipation.

'And about the good life,' Madhavan Nair said, 'I suppose we have to explore . . . .'

'Ask your Maeshtar to go and fall at his feet. I shall take care of the rest.'

The Khazi who came in for a cup of tea was told of the anonymous petition.

'Foul lies!' the Khazi said, 'Treachery!'

'We will meet higher officers if need be,' said the gentle Aliyar flaring up, 'we will give affidavits.'

'An anonymous petition!' the Khazi said. 'Verily, Sayed Mian Sheikh will not permit this.'

'But the Inspeatar permits this,' the peon said unthinkingly, and was seized with terror the very next moment. He stole a fleeting glance at the mountain—it wore an ominous hood of clouds, and seemed more formidable than all the clerks of the Inspectorate put together. He left, sorely disturbed at this new intrusion by a spirit. On his walk home he chanted the ten names of Arjuna for protection against lightning, he looked over his shoulder to make sure he wasn't haunted . . . . The little crowd at Aliyar's stayed on. The Khazi's anger had not cooled; he muttered to himself, 'Which dog has done this?'

'Let it be anybody,' the tailor said, 'And Aliyar, I go on credit. Two appams, two steamed bananas—'

Aliyar smiled. 'Let it be on Aliyar. Mollakka would have called it Allah's credit.'

Ravi returned. He had been away ten days, a solid third of a month of unexplained absence. It was a pause in the rain, and Appu-Kili was wandering along the fringes of the village. He caught sight of Ravi and came prancing to the seedling house.

'Etto!' he cried in the joy of reunion, 'whe ha yu been?'

'To Kashi, my pet,' Ravi said.

As he mopped the rain water from Appu's hair, Ravi choked for a moment. The touch of the cretin's hair brought back vivid memories—the Aryans and the reborn children, the karmic lice lost in grief.

'Did anyone tease you when I was away?'

'Pootham. He beat wid umb'ella.'

'Don't worry. We will drive him away. Now, here is something for my Parrot.'

Appu-Kili grabbed the packet of chocolates from Ravi with grunts of thanksgiving.

'Etto,' he said, 'catch you goo big daagon fie.'

'Where have you been, Maash?'

Madhavan Nair was settled comfortably on a bench, while Ravi unpacked his bag.

'Where have you been?' the tailor asked again.

'To Kashi,' Ravi jested.

'All the manes doing well?'

Then, with great circumspection, lest he upset his friend, Madhavan Nair told Ravi all about the latest plot against the school.

'Don't be upset, Maash. The whole village is united—'

'But, Madhavan Nair, I'm not upset.'

'If the Board closes down the school, we have worked out alternatives.'

Ravi was not listening, his mind was on the cockroaches which had come meekly by their inheritance; he had returned again to violate their mildewed spaces. I am sorry, my little brethren, said Ravi. Children burdened themselves with reading and reckoning here, and I sought a Sarai, a place of rest on a long, long journey. A black hairy spider which had returned to the seedling house during the absence of its human resident raced on the wall in circles, dismayed. I intruded on this Sarai, said Ravi, for too long, desecrating its primeval nights with lamps and incense, while Time, untamed and awesome, cried beyond the timepieces, cried out as dark blue winds. Roach and spider lay in wait in these winds.

'I was wondering, Maash . . . ' said Madhavan Nair, 'A visit to the Inspector's office, an apology, a settlement.'

Ravi said gently, 'No.'

Madhavan Nair struggled to find words, 'But . . . Khasak has taken decisions . . . .'

They would raise the money needed for a school of their own, and the communists of Kozhanasseri would teach them how to organize a committee.

The day after, the comrades came to the seedling house.

Ravi was telling Appu-Kili a story.

'We are from Kozhanasseri—'

'Welcome, comrades.'

One of them was thin as a leaf, and the other dark and stocky as a mountain troll.

'I work with peasants' unions,' the thin one said. 'Sankaran is the name.'

'Kanni Moothan,' the troll said. 'Secretary of Kozhanasseri's Peace Council.'

'Happy meeting you, comrades. And to know there is a peace council close by. What does the council do anyway?'

'Oh, nothing in particular. Occasionally we outlaw nuclear war. Right now our concern is the school—'

'It is a conspiracy,' the thin comrade put in. 'We shall deal with it.'

Appu-Kili did not like the story being interrupted.

'Etto,' he said, 'thel shtoyi.'

The Parrot could not take a story in instalments. So, to spare him the discomfort, Ravi said, 'The story is over.'

The cretin stood before Ravi and the comrades, sullen and dejected, then moved on to the verandah to watch the water run down the eaves. The story had ended without meaning or resolution.

The comrades were telling Ravi another story. Of Kelan the compradore bourgeois, Sivaraman Nair the feudalist, of the peon from the bureaucracy.

'There is no national bourgeoisie here,' Kanni Moothan concluded his class analysis. 'Khasak is a fortress of reaction.'

'National bourgeoisie?' Ravi asked. 'What is that?'

'I was speaking generally. For example, the outcaste women are not allowed to wear blouses while transplanting the paddy seedlings. Just imagine! Women stooping bare-breasted—'

'I can imagine,' said Ravi. 'Must be gorgeous.'

The words were spoken in play, and sensing the awkardness, he tried to explain it away. He said, 'I was speaking generally.'

That made it even worse, and ruined the conversation. The comrades rose after an abrupt tailpiece, 'Maash, you should be in the forefront.'

'Very well.'

Later, in the Mosque of the King—

'Comrade—'

The visitors were promptly corrected, 'Call me Khazi.'

'Ah, yes,' the peasant said, 'Our Khazi is no stranger to the situation.'

'Of course not,' the Khazi said.

'It's a conspiracy.'

'What doubt is there?'

'Imperialist forces are at work,' the troll said, 'We in the peace movement know it only too well.'

'Be not afraid!' said the Khazi, and chanted a spell against imperialism leaving the comrades mildly disconcerted.

'The movement would be greatly strengthened by the Khazi's return—'

The Khazi ended the chant with the mystic *al fateha*. The comrades grew nervous in the haunted mosque.

The rain mingled with the steam of the earth and curtained off the seedling house. Kunhamina came through mist and rain, with a tiffin carrier.

'Umma sends this, Saar,' she said, 'patthiri and meat curry.'

'Sit down, my little one,' said Ravi. She wouldn't sit. As in days gone by she came and stood close. Ravi took her hands in his. His thoughts went to the girl bewildered by herself on the peak of Chetali, to the covenant of the mountain. She swayed closer, now she was seated on his lap, her eyes brimming with tears.

'They say you are going away,' she said, 'Is that true, Saar?'

Ravi laid his hand over her head in blessing.

'Won't you come back, Saar?'

The fish with a silver crest and red spots hibernated in the crevices of Chetali for long years, said the villagers. This was the messenger of the Sheikh, and he swam down in times of elemental catastrophies. On an evening when the rain let up, bathers in the brook saw the crested one.

The great wind began the next night. For two nights and two days it blew without mercy, it blew the thatches away, while children cried and their parents prayed. Black palms were uprooted, sturdy tamarind branches torn away.

Then both wind and rain calmed. In that gentle interlude, Ravi and Madhavan Nair took a walk on the hills. Khaṣak lay wrapped in the sunset, cleansed, dry. The sky hung low, holding back its colossal power. Neither the teacher nor the tailor spoke of the school.

'Where will Kili sleep, Madhavan Nair?'

'In my shop, Maash.'

They began their walk back. They had a glimpse of the fugitive village.

'I can't believe Kodacchi is dead,' Ravi said, reminiscing. 'What a name! What did you say it meant?'

'Woman of the mountain mists.'

Fringes of conversation. Trivia. They kept themselves away from its core. They spoke of fireworks and films.

They parted at the gate of the seedling house. Ravi opened the gate and went in. Madhavan Nair walked over the rise into the village. Neither of them looked back.

Madhavan Nair felt an impulse to go back, to be with Ravi a little longer. Meetings and partings, the torn shreds of Time . . . .

Ravi rose early. It was still the hour of the Morning Star. He took care not to wake up Appu-Kili who was fast asleep in the corridor. Ravi kept the corridor open and came back to the two rooms of the seedling house. He slipped his letter of resignation into the attendance register. He had told Madhavan Nair not to come, he didn't want a farewell. The key to the school could be found on the door-frame.

Ravi stood before the locked door for a moment, eyes closed, prayerful. Father! he said. Father of my eventides, my twilight journeys, allow me to go. I leave this nest of sewn leaves, nest of rebirth.

Ravi walked out, his meagre belongings in a satchel. The rain fell on his outspread umbrella, it fell first in a mere patter, then drummed on the taut tafetta. The rain grew heavier, the monsoon rain without thunder and lightning . . . . Ravi reached Koomankavu.

The rain was a steady downpour, a low dome of white opacity. The storm had been more savage in Koomankavu, the mounted shacks had all been blown away, and no one, nothing, moved in what had once been a little bazar . . . . There was still time for the bus to come. Ravi surveyed the scene of the great quiet and stood near the bus shelter, now a heap of sodden clods. He played with the clods, prising them apart with his feet.

Ravi looked with fond curiosity at the little blue and black apparition that slithered out of the clods. The blue-black one looked up at Ravi, conversing with its flickering tongue. Ravi saw the tiny hood, outspread now. Infant fangs pierced Ravi's foot. Teething, my little one?

With a last playful flick of its forked tongue, the snake

slid back into the alleys of wet earth.

The rain, nothing but the rain. White, opaque. The rain slept, it dreamt. Ravi lay down. He smiled. The waters of the Timeless Rain touched him. Grass sprouted through the pores of his body. Above him the great rain shrank small as a thumb, the size of the departing subtle body.

Ravi lay waiting for the bus.

An Afterword

IT WAS AN almost magical journey. The villagers of Thasarak were giving me a reception decades after the success of my book *Khasakkinte Itihasam*, translated here as *The Legends of Khasak*. For one evening in their drab existence they were no longer the peasants they were, but characters waiting to felicitate their author, faery people opening the portals for their conjuror. We drove along the bank of the irrigation canal, an interminable journey, mystic, wonderful; even the scarlet sunset seemed a seal on the time-warp of Khasak.

It had all begun this way: in 1956 my sister had got a teaching assignment in the village of Thasarak, a state scheme that sent barefoot graduates to man single-teacher schools in backward villages.

Since it was hard for a single girl to be on her own in a remote village, my parents had rented a little farmhouse and moved in with my sister. Meanwhile I had been sacked from the college where I taught. So jobless and at a loose end, I too had joined them in Thasarak, to drown my sorrows in the countryside.

I had grown up in the countryside, mountain country in fact, where my father had commanded a hilltop camp of the armed constabulary. There were no good schools within manageable distance, and even the primary school of the Moplahs (Muslims) in the valley, which I had eventually joined, was a rundown outfit. And the climb up and down the hill was too much for me—I was a frail child—so I had dropped out and sailed through my childhood on fairy tales. Destiny had been readying me for Khasak.

Towards the end of my days in the college, I happened to share a platform with the President of the Malabar District Board at a teachers' meet. After the function the President offered to drop me back home, and during that drive we began talking of new writing in Malayalam. Both of us were communists, card-carriers, and naturally we began a dreadful class analysis. I had published two long stories depicting imaginary peasant uprisings in Palghat; commenting on them the Comrade-President said, 'They were good stories, but I wish you could write something with more Inquilab* in it.'

That precisely was what was occupying my mind then. Revolution. I was familiar with the Palghat countryside with its landscape of paddies and its hilarious dialects. I could put together a hundred episodes with ease, choose from a dozen locations. The city-bred schoolmaster coming to the village was almost a made-to-order catalyst. I told the Comrade-President that I was working on something, and wanted to fine-hone my pilgrim-revolutionary to perfection. He was pleased and said he would wait for the book.

It was then that tragedy from afar shattered the carnival of liberation. In Hungary, they tricked and shot Imre Nagy. It blew my mind. I turned away, I began my uncharted journey.

---

* revolution

Looking back, I thank Providence, because I missed writing the 'revolutionary' novel by a hair's breadth. Had I written it, I would have merely made one more boring entry in Marxism's futile, repetitive bibliography.

And then I was gasping for fresh air, a whole skyful of living breath. Polemics, even history, did not matter anymore. I plumped for plants and flowers, and a place like Khasak. Destiny was in command, Khasak was waiting.

Once the spell was broken the rest was easy. The Stalinist claustrophobia melted away as though it had never existed. Ravi, my hero, liberation's germ-carrier, now came to the village and re-entered his enchanted childhood. He was no longer the teacher, in atonement he would *learn*. He would learn from the stupor of Khasak.

With that decision the architecture of the novel changed, the language changed, in a way that surprised even me. They say that the Malayalam language, has never been the same again. I cannot vouch for that, but certainly the book taught me this—no language, however physically confined, however historically deprived, is left without springheads of regeneration. There is as much narrative potential in Malayalam as in the imperial languages. Khasak has given that assurance to successor generations.

I have strayed into the theory of post-decolonization diglossia without intending to. Let me get back to the story of Khasak, not the legends.

Thasarak, as Malayalam place-names go, was a quaint and unusual name. It was mesmeric—maybe with my rejection of materialism I was in the right state of internal enchantment to be mesmerized. I coined the fictional name, equally out of the ordinary—*Khasak*. A few other names haunted me as well. Allah-pitcha, the mullah, and of course Sayed Mian Sheikh, the spirit-guardian of Khasak, which I improvised from the name of the djinn the Khazi invoked during seances.

The djinn bore the name Sayed Sheikh Hassan Mastan and resided in Arabian oases. Within days of my coming to Thasarak I had made friends with both the Khazi and the mullah. It was a remarkable innocence that made the Khazi let me into the hermetic secrets of Thasarak. He began telling me one day how difficult it was for the Sheikh to travel all the way from Arabia to the supplicant devotee in Thasarak.

'Spirits of evil,' the Khazi said 'their evil eyes have to be shut. The Sheikh blindfolds them.'

The Khazi grew conjectural when the story touched corporeal details, beginning with his first encounter. I corrected him on a few slips, but that didn't matter in the perennial epic of Khasak. The incongruities caused no embarrassment. Will the Newtonian physicist be upset by the Einsteinian equation? Truth is light splintered through a prism and that gave me the idea of the astrophysicist who turns away from the outer universe to the space within. The Khazi's sorcery was no less tenable than the Big Bang theory. What obtained in Thasarak was a playful interface between being and beyond being.

This interface was all that Thasarak contributed to *The Legends of Khasak*. The rest was the routine work of the fabulist. But that one contribution was enormous, it restored my freedom to mourn for Imre Nagy.

Another contribution, less apparent then, was the villagers' attitude to time, which even as I succumbed to it, I confused with the lethargy of my own joblessness. But no. It was a positive input. The people of Thasarak were in no hurry. Theirs was another Time, the duration of faster-than-light tachaeons come home to rest.

In that sense *The Legends of Khasak* is a ballad of re-enchantment. Lots of visitors come now to Thasarak—academics, young and curious people, the book's cult readership. If they come looking for the Khasak software they are bound to go back disappointed, because the *Legends* is not the story of Thasarak.

The villagers themselves do not mind this attention. The Malayalam original shot into prominence many years ago, and even today it is a best seller. The villagers too have kept the happenings alive. They are lost in a kind of collective narcissism. As I walked into the reception long years after my eventless stay in Thasarak, a Muslim youth crushed me with a hug, he was crying.

'Kili-Annan,' he sobbed. 'is dead.' My character Appu-Kili, a prop of the novel, was created after no Thasarakkian model. He was the embodiment of a childhood memory. But I did not want to violate the villager's boon of love.

Practically every villager has identified some situation which gives him or her entry into the fictional personae. The Khazi, now the Imam of the prosperous mosque in Palghat town, summed it up for me. 'After all,' he said, 'these things are willed by God.'

Indeed they are. As I stood up in the dusk to talk to the semi-literate audience that filled the tiny yard, I sensed the ballad of Khasak emanating from them, infinitely richer than anything I could create and celebrate. I recalled too the handbill they had printed for the occasion. In it they had designated me the beloved son of Thasarak.

Son indeed, merciful Allah! The beloved son in whom You are well pleased.